God, help me.

Rett waited a few ̶ ̶ ̶ ̶ ̶ ̶ ̶ ̶ ̶ much of a break as ̶ ̶ ̶ ̶ ̶ ̶ ̶ ̶ ̶ ̶ ̶ ̶ ̶ ̶ he had a villain to chase. At last he retied his cloth and stood up. "Time to go."

To her credit, Elizabeth didn't complain. Just stretched her arms, rubbed her back a bit and climbed into the saddle like an old pro. He couldn't help but notice as she mounted the horse that she wore denim pants under her skirts. *She must be sweltering.* "You're going to have to shed the skirts or the pants. You'll pass out if you don't."

"Why don't you let me worry about me, Ranger Smith? Concern yourself with finding Hardy and freeing my brother." She tossed her head, a look of defiance in her eyes that said she'd never do a thing as long as he was the one who suggested it. Then she calmly drew up Lucy's reins as if she'd been waiting on him rather than the other way around.

He'd never met a more exasperating woman in his life.

Renae Brumbaugh is a bestselling author and contributor to many books, and she writes an award-winning newspaper humor column. She's also a happy wife and mother in Texas, where she wears boots, raises chickens and tries to be rugged without breaking a fingernail. Learn more about Renae and her books at renaebrumbaugh.com.

RENAE BRUMBAUGH

Lone Star Ranger

HEARTSONG
PRESENTS

Recycling programs
for this product may
not exist in your area.

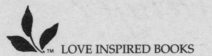 LOVE INSPIRED BOOKS

ISBN-13: 978-0-373-48768-4

Lone Star Ranger

Copyright © 2015 by Renae Brumbaugh

Delight yourself in the Lord,
and He will give you the desires of your heart.
Commit your way to the Lord; trust in Him, and
He will act. He will bring forth your righteousness
as the light, and your justice as the noonday.
—*Psalms* 37:4–6

To my husband, Rick, who is to me a living, breathing example of Christ's love, and who inspires me to be more than I thought I could be. And in honor of my late grandfather, Everett Smith, a real Texas Ranger and one of my favorite heroes. Most of all, to God, who continues to bless me beyond belief.

Chapter 1

August, 1877

Elizabeth Covington inhaled the scent of freshly baked bread as the hansom driver pulled into Houston's Market Square. Before, when her brother, Evan, had suggested breakfast, she'd turned her nose up. But now, with that robust aroma wafting through her senses...now she was hungry. "Let's eat over there, in the Kennedy Trading Center. I heard someone on the train say their restaurant and bakery is worthwhile."

"Finally," Evan answered. "I'm famished."

"You're always famished," she countered as Evan assisted her from the carriage.

As she climbed down, Elizabeth noticed the hansom driver staring, though he seemed more focused on Evan than on her. Odd. Most people noticed her height.

At five foot eleven, she knew she was a spectacle, but she'd long since passed the time when she cared.

The ogling and whispering continued as they made their way through the restaurant. Funny how much attention her height drew, as if she were a circus exhibit. She looked people in the eye and smiled, part challenge, part mischief. She secretly relished the looks of embarrassment on their faces when they knew they'd been caught gawking. Served them right.

Oh, well. Since she couldn't follow her dreams of becoming a lawyer like her father and brother, due to the tiny little matter of being female, she figured she could always make a living in a carnival sideshow.

Papa. The thought of him brought another unexpected pang. How many months had he been gone now? Six? Nearly seven. How she missed him.

Once they were seated at a table, Elizabeth rolled her ankles back and forth under her skirts and once again wished she were a man. Their shoes were so much more sensible.

"Evan, why don't we purchase land here in Texas?"

He set aside his menu. "Have you decided to become a rancher now?"

She wanted to kick him under the table. Would have if they'd been at home. "So what if I have? I like it here. It's rugged. You know I've never fit into that prissy Boston society life. Papa never wanted me to. Here I could wear dungarees and ride a horse and do as I please."

"Well...I don't know about buying a ranch. But I was thinking this morning that Houston probably needs a good law office. I've only noticed one, but the town is growing and could surely support another."

"Really? You're thinking of moving here?" Several customers turned to look at her, and she reminded herself to speak quietly.

"I'm considering it. Of course, I'd need your assistance."

"You'd let me practice law?"

"You know better. I'd be a laughingstock, and the practice would fail."

"But you can't argue like I can. You know I'm better at litigation."

"Which is precisely why I'd need your assistance. But you know you can't argue in court. It's not allowed. It's not even legal, Elizabeth."

There was a small commotion at the restaurant entrance, but Elizabeth wouldn't be distracted. "I've heard people are more open-minded here."

Evan held the menu again, pretending to study it, but she knew better. She decided to drop the matter for now. "Where is the waiter?" she asked under her breath.

The commotion grew louder, and they both strained in their seats to see what was happening. It was the hansom driver. He held some sort of paper and looked through the crowd, examining each face. A tall man in a cowboy hat, wearing a badge, followed close behind. At last the driver's gaze landed on Evan. "There he is! That's him!"

The cowboy studied the flyer, then looked at Evan and pushed between the tables until he stood before them. His hand rested on his holster in an unspoken threat. "Good day, Mr. Hardy. You're under arrest for the murder of more than two dozen people. Would you come with me, please?"

* * *

Rett's heart pounded, and he wondered if the man in front of him could sense it. He tightened his grasp on the pistol, expecting to have to use it at any moment and praying he wouldn't be forced to. After all the tracking, all the killings, all the narrow escapes, could it really be this simple?

It was him, no doubt about it. As soon as the cab-driver pointed him out, Rett knew. He'd referred to the face on the flyer to be sure, and any doubts had been removed. The man seated near the window was none other than James Weston Hardy, one of the most wanted criminals in the United States.

"Excuse me?" Hardy asked. Rett hadn't expected him to sound so…refined. Yet of course he would. The man was no idiot. His intelligence had kept him a free man for far too long. "I believe there's been some mistake."

"No mistake. Now stand up."

The man just sat there, his mouth agape. Rett had to hand it to him—he was a pretty good actor. He pulled his gun from its holster but kept it pointed downward, and the people around them gasped.

"I beg your pardon! Put that thing away!" The woman seated across from Hardy stood to her feet. She was a tall one. What was her part in this ruse? Hardy was known as a womanizer. Surely she'd been taken in, just as many others had.

Keeping his eyes on Hardy, he said, "Ma'am, please take your seat. I don't know what he's told you, but your companion here is a cold-blooded killer. Mr. Hardy, I said stand up!" The force in his voice brought the man out of his seat, and Rett aimed the pistol right at his chest. "Turn around."

Surprisingly, Hardy did as he was told, and Rett cuffed him tight.

"Stop! You're hurting him!" The woman reached for Hardy, but Rett put himself between her and the killer. "I'm sorry, ma'am, but you need to stay out of this, or I'll be forced to arrest you, too."

Hardy craned his neck toward the woman. "Elizabeth. Go to the hotel and get my case. My papers—I can prove my identity."

"Yes, certainly. We'll get this straightened out in no time," the woman said, then snatched the flyer from where it had fallen on the table and turned a glare on Rett that looked madder than a skillet full of rattlesnakes. "And once we do, you will be held accountable for this public humiliation. Where are you taking my brother?"

Well-spoken and fiery. Not bad to look at, either. She was only about three or four inches shorter than Rett, and he wondered how long she'd been hooked up with Hardy. The last woman Hardy had been associated with was described as petite. Now she was dead. "I'm takin' him to the county jail, ma'am. You're welcome to follow along if you like. But if I were you, I'd stay as far away from this fellow as possible."

"Well, you're not me, and that's not the man you're looking for. Where is the jail?" She tagged along behind as Rett urged Hardy forward, ignoring the stares and whispers. He couldn't believe he actually had James Weston Hardy in custody. And only his fourth month as a Ranger. Wait till Cody and Ray found out.

"Follow me."

"I can't follow you, you big...you big imbecile! You heard Evan. I need to retrieve his things."

Nice vocabulary. She was smart, too, and clearly devoted to Hardy. This one bore watching. Once they reached the entrance to Market Square, he stopped, keeping a solid grasp on Hardy. "It's not far. Why don't you come with me now, and once we get your brother all settled, I'll escort you to your hotel. Fair enough?"

A slight nod was her only answer. Hardy gave no struggle, but then, he wouldn't. He was too smart for that. Despite his meek appearance and demeanor, Rett knew this man was a cold-blooded killer.

Elizabeth sat in a crude chair against the wall of the sheriff's office and watched as the lawman escorted Evan into another part of the building. As much as she wanted to put up a fight, she knew she'd best serve her brother by holding her tongue. Papa had taught her that. Watch and learn. Observe everything. You never knew when you'd learn something you could use to your advantage in court.

Papa. How she missed him. Though he'd made it clear she was expected to conduct herself like a lady when in court or around his professional associates, he'd allowed her the freedom to be herself most of the time. He'd valued her judgment.

She could just hear him laugh as she played devil's advocate. She often helped him prepare for trial in that way, anticipating the opposing party's strategies and arguments. More than once he'd credited her with a win.

But now he was gone. She couldn't wire him to

come fix this travesty of justice. Imagine Evan a murderer! Absurd.

The flyer was crumpled in her hand; she'd nearly forgotten it. Carefully, she smoothed it out and studied the image.

Oh, my.

It did look like Evan. Except for…something around the eyes was different. Beneath the drawing it said "James Weston Hardy—Dead or Alive."

Elizabeth's free hand flew to her face as she stifled a gasp. Dead or alive! What if…what if the man had shot on sight? As if he heard her thoughts, the door swung open and the lawman crossed the room toward her.

"It will be a few more minutes, Miss— I'm sorry. I didn't catch your name."

Elizabeth stood. "Miss Covington. Elizabeth Covington. And the man you've falsely accused of being a ruthless killer is my brother, Evan Covington. He happens to be one of the kindest, gentlest men on the planet."

The man looked to be about Evan's age. Twenty-six, twenty-seven maybe. The skin around his eyes crinkled in a way she might have found attractive if she hadn't already found him loathsome. "Well, ma'am. I'm not sure how to respond. You say he's your brother, Evan. But James Weston Hardy has been on the run from the law. He's been spotted in this area recently. And your so-called brother fits his description perfectly."

"I'm aware of that." Elizabeth glanced at the flyer again while she pushed down a wave of temper. A hysterical woman certainly wouldn't do Evan any good.

"I can see the resemblance." She looked at the man and realized he hadn't given her his name. "But you're wrong, Mr. ..."

"Smith. Rett Smith, of the Texas Rangers." He offered his hand, and she reluctantly took it. No use alienating the man. Papa's words surfaced in her memory: *Know your strengths. If you want to win in court, you must use every gift God has given you. Every one.* Well, she might not be in court, but she knew her strengths. And as much as she hated to, she decided to call on every available...gift?

Elizabeth batted her eyelashes, blinked twice and let the tiniest sigh escape. Not enough to make her seem totally helpless, but enough to call upon his male need to be the protector. "Well, Ranger Smith. After looking at the image on the flyer, I don't blame you at all. But if you'll just escort me back to the hotel, I can save you further trouble. I can produce proof of my brother's identification."

"As I said, Miss Covington, I'll gladly escort you back to your hotel." It was working! "If you'll be seated again, I'll be with you in about an hour."

An hour? So much for womanly charm. "I see. Well, thank you, sir, but I simply can't wait that long. I suppose I can find my way on my own."

"I don't advise that, Miss Covington. Houston is a nice town, but we've got some rough characters around these parts. If I were you, I'd wait right there."

Facing away from him, she let a smile creep across her face, then fought it back as she turned. "Thank you for your advice, Ranger Smith, but I'm afraid I have no choice. I refuse to sit here and calmly wait while you do who knows what to an innocent man, especially when that man is my brother." She spun around, and the click-click of her shoes echoed in the room as she headed for the door. It had a nice effect, and she expected him to follow her at any moment.

She pushed open the door and glanced back, but he didn't follow.

She continued to the corner, past a mishmash of people representing many races and economic stations. Still no Ranger Smith.

She stopped, looked one way, then the other and tried to get her bearings. Still no Ranger Smith.

Someone jostled her from behind, and she spun around. "Pardon me, ma'am." A man wearing suspenders, a stained shirt and a foul odor spoke directly into her left ear, and his breath nearly sent her into the street. She backed away, watching her step so as not to land in any horse droppings, and the man continued on his way.

Still no Mr. Smith. She'd felt sure his heroic lawman ego would take over and send him to her rescue. "I must get those papers," she muttered. "Poor Evan! I know the hotel is around here somewhere... Is it two blocks over? Three? And then to the left. No... right. Oh, bother."

"Miss Covington."

How she could be so relieved to hear the voice of a man she loathed, she didn't know. But relieved she was. "Oh, Ranger Smith. I thought you were unavailable to escort me. It's so kind of you to take time away from your busy schedule, but I do thank you. Evan and I are staying at the Houston Hotel." She took his elbow and waited expectantly for him to lead the way, but he didn't move. Just looked at her, with... Goodness. Sunlight glistened off golden hair that lay in a tumbled mess on the Ranger's head. And his eyes were… Oh, those eyes. Why hadn't she noticed them before? She lifted a gloved hand to shield the glare as the sun glinted off the most brilliant green eyes she'd ever seen.

Chapter 2

Rett tried to size up the woman before him, watched her back away from a dockworker who looked as though he'd imbibed a few too many spirits. His gut told him Elizabeth was no criminal, though why she'd lie about Hardy being her brother was a mystery. The criminal did come from a large family...and they were known to hide him from time to time. Still, even if she was his sister, she'd lied about the name.

But she wasn't his sister. Back at the sheriff's office, Rett had looked over the James Weston Hardy file. Though he had sisters in Texas, both were short, plump and in their thirties.

He couldn't afford to let this woman out of his sight. With Hardy securely behind bars, he decided to leave the outlaw with the sheriff and stay close to Miss... Covington. He tipped his hat to her and said, "Forgive me, Miss Covington. I don't know where my manners were. Of course I'll escort you. Right this way, ma'am."

Before long they stood in the lobby of the Houston Hotel. "I'll be right down," she told him, and he wondered for a moment if he should let her go to her room alone.

"I'll be waiting," he told her. He couldn't let on that he was suspicious of her. Not yet, anyway. Maybe he could follow at a distance. Halfway up the staircase, she turned and smiled at him, and he nodded as he stood there holding his hat.

As soon as she left his sight, he crammed the hat back onto his head and took the stairs two at a time. Once on the second floor, he stayed in the shadows. There she was! Just entering the third room to the left. The door clicked shut, and he moved down the hallway until he could read the room number. Room 217.

A tall, leafy plant in an ornate pot stood against one wall. He scooted close to it and tried to remain inconspicuous. His heart still thumped a little too fast at the thought of arresting James Weston Hardy. Not that he'd done anything heroic or out of the ordinary. A driver spotted Hardy, reported him to Rett, and Rett simply followed through as he'd been trained to do.

The story of his life, really. He'd come to be a Ranger quite by accident. Why, just because he'd chased a man at a train station who'd snatched a woman's reticule. Anyone would have done the same! After an arrest was made, the sheriff in town had asked where Rett was headed. When he learned Rett was looking for work on the railroad, the man told him the Rangers were looking for recruits and wrote him a letter of recom-

mendation right then and there. Little did Rett know at
the time how hard it was to be accepted as a Ranger.

He turned his attention back to the day's events.
Something didn't seem quite right about the whole
thing. Hardy was known to be violent. According to
his profile, every time a lawman drew near, Hardy
came out shooting. Why was today different? The
man had politely protested, then complied with Rett's
orders. Was this some sort of trick? Did Hardy have
something up his sleeve?

A door to his right clicked open and a well-dressed
silver-haired woman entered the hallway. "Ma'am," he
said. He tipped his hat, then, remembering his manners, removed it.

The woman eyed his badge, then let her eyes travel
the length of him, disapproval dripping from her coun-
tenance. "Are you a sheriff?" she asked.

"No, ma'am. I'm a Texas Ranger." He was used to
mixed reactions. Though people were always glad to
have a lawman around when they needed one, not all
of them wanted to spend time with them when they
didn't need to. And especially the Rangers. Most people respected the Rangers, but it could be a grudg-
ing respect. Some saw the group of law enforcers as
renegades, as infringing on the local justice system.

"I see. Don't you have some Indians to shoot?"

"Not today."

"I see." The woman adjusted her spectacles and
continued on her way. Rett was still looking after
the woman when Elizabeth stepped into the hallway
carrying a black case. Surprise turned to annoyance
before she masked her feelings with a loaded-pistol

smile. "How…sweet of you to come after me, Mr. Smith."

He bit back a clever retort and offered his arm instead. "I hope you found what you need."

"Yes, I believe I did." She took his arm, and together they descended the stairs and walked the short way back to the station. He didn't bother to tell her no amount of paperwork would do any good. The authorities would not, under any circumstances, release the man they believed to be James Weston Hardy. It would take a lot more than a few pieces of paper to bring his freedom. It would take an all-out miracle. More than likely, Miss Elizabeth Covington's brother, beau or whoever he was would hang within the week.

The bigger question now was whether or not the woman beside him would view that hanging as a free woman or from behind bars.

Elizabeth pushed down the urge to punch the sheriff in the nose. As for that Ranger, he was no help at all. He just sat there. For the fourth time, she pointed at Evan's name on the Harvard Law School diploma. "This is a legitimate diploma, sir. And if you won't accept this, just look at his correspondence. Why would he carry around letters addressed to Evan Covington unless they belong to him?"

"Tell me again how you came to be traveling with Mr. Hardy," the sheriff repeated.

They were getting nowhere. She glared at the man and clamped her lips together to keep from saying something she'd regret. Her papa's oft-repeated Scripture surfaced in her memory: *"For the wrath of man worketh not the righteousness of God."* It wouldn't help Evan if they threw her in jail alongside him.

"I don't know how many times I must repeat myself. He's not Mr. Hardy. He's my brother." She used her finger to draw an invisible line beneath his name on the document. "Evan Covington. He recently graduated from law school. Several months before that, we lost our papa. Evan thought it might be nice to take a trip, just the two of us, before he settled into his law career."

Finally, the sheriff took the paper and studied it. When he answered, his tone was even more patronizing than before. "Look, miss, we've been through this. I don't know what he's told you, but the man you claim is your brother is actually one of the meanest men on the planet. Why, he once shot a man just for snoring."

"The man you have in custody is indeed my brother, and he wouldn't hurt anyone. As for your tale about shooting a man for snoring, that sounds more like legend than reality."

"It's true." Rett Smith stepped forward. For the past few minutes, he'd sat behind one of the desks and studied a couple of the letters she'd brought. At least he appeared to give the documents some consideration. "Hardy shot multiple times through the wall of his hotel room because the snores from the next room kept him from sleeping."

How dreadful. No wonder they were determined to hold Evan, if they thought he was Hardy. And truly, the resemblance was uncanny.

Things were not looking good. Not at all.

"May I speak with my brother, please?"

"I'm afraid that's not possible, ma'am. Your brother,

if that's who he is, has the right to an attorney. There's a law office down the street. If you really want to help him, I suggest you go find some legal counsel." There was that patronizing tone again, and Elizabeth decided once and for all she did not like that sheriff.

The Ranger seemed more tolerable, even if he had been the one to arrest Evan. At least he appeared to listen to her. "Which direction?" she asked.

"Four doors down, to the left," the sheriff said as he held the diploma up to the light. "Look at this, Everett. It's got gold letters and everything. Hardy went to a lot of trouble to get this made."

Everett. Elizabeth took note of the flush on the back of the Ranger's neck, the slight clamping of his jaw. So Rett was short for Everett. The sheriff—she still didn't know his name—wrinkled the document in his chubby hand. "Be careful with that!" she cried and snatched it from him.

The sheriff laughed at her. Laughed at her! "I suppose with him being a lawyer and all, he might refuse his right to counsel."

"That's enough, Tom," Rett said under his breath.

She'd had enough of both of these men. Elizabeth gathered the papers and slid them back into the case she'd given Evan as a graduation gift. "If you're quite done, Sheriff—" she fought the desire to call him by his given name, Tom "—I'll be on my way."

"You go right ahead, ma'am. Tell him Sheriff Goodman sent you."

Good man. How ironic. The sheriff stood, and Elizabeth relished a bit of satisfaction at the fact that she had a good three inches on the man. He tilted his head back, and this time, she didn't even try to restrain the condescension in her smirk. "Good day, Sheriff. You'll be hearing from Evan's attorney shortly." She leaned toward him a bit as she said the word *shortly*, and Rett let out a chuckle, then coughed as if to cover it.

With that, she lifted her chin, spun around and left them. She squinted against the bright sunlight, and her feet stepped in rapid pace with her heart. Evan was in trouble, and she wasn't sure how best to help him. *Oh, Papa. I wish you were here.* How she wished she could send a wire to her Papa. He could fix all of this. His associate had moved to Chicago soon after Papa's death. No, not Chicago. Somewhere near Chicago. But she didn't know how to track him down.

She soon stood in front of the law office of Stanley Herrington, which was in need of a paint job. Perhaps the man was so busy defending his clients he didn't have time to keep up repairs. A bell jangled overhead as she pushed open the door and was assaulted by a wall of cigar smoke. The smoke, coupled with the difference in lighting, had a blinding effect.

"What can I do for ya?" called a rough voice through the haze.

"Um—" Cough! "I...I am Elizabeth Covington, and my brother, Evan, is in need of legal assistance." Tears spilled down her cheeks, whether from frustration or the smoke, she wasn't sure. She blinked, trying to see through the haze.

"Come in and shut the door. You're lettin' the flies in."

She stepped inside, just enough to let the door close behind her. She couldn't breathe. Her stomach tensed with a mixture of nausea and frustration, and she still couldn't see the face attached to the voice.

A hand thrust toward her, and she took it. Strong

handshake. That was a good sign. "Stanley Herrington, at your service. Sit down and tell me what your brother's done."

She sat in the only chair she could see. Feeling around in her reticule, she realized she'd misplaced her handkerchief. A great sigh heaved from her chest, and she was immediately sorry, for the smoke burned her chest and lungs. Her throat felt raw as she spoke, and her voice sounded husky. "He hasn't done anything. He's innocent."

"I see. Well, why don't you tell me what he's been accused of?" The man set his cigar on a tray, and the fog finally cleared enough for her to make out a bald man leaning back in his chair. His collar was undone, and he wore a jacket that looked as if it might have fit a year ago. A mound of belly spilled over his belt, and he breathed with a slight wheeze.

"I'm afraid it's a case of mistaken identity. Evan bears a strong resemblance to a wanted criminal, and he's being held in the jail, just a few doors down."

"Which criminal does he look like?"

Elizabeth tried to clear her throat, but it just made it hurt more. "The name on the flyer read James Weston Hardy."

Herrington let out an expletive, then leaned forward in his chair. "Miss Covington, do you know how serious this is? James Weston Hardy is the most wanted, most hunted criminal in these parts. Perhaps in the United States. If they think they've got him, he'll hang within the week."

She wanted to breathe. Wanted to respond. But the breath just wouldn't come. *Oh, dear God,* she prayed. *I don't know what to do.*

This man was her only hope. She silently compared Stanley Herrington to her dignified papa. To her polished, mannerly brother. Why, to hire this man to represent Evan could be a death sentence in itself. "My brother is a lawyer—a Harvard graduate. Our papa was one of Boston's leading lawyers. He allowed me to assist him on many of his cases. Perhaps together we could…" Her mind had too many thoughts at once, and she took a moment to sort her ideas into manageable pieces.

"Did you hear me, Miss Covington?"

Oh, dear. He'd been talking, and she'd missed most of what he'd said. "I'm sorry. I guess I was lost in thought."

"I said I'll do it, on one condition."

"What's that?"

"You stay out of my way and let me handle things."

"But I can help. I think you'll find my knowledge of the law is extensive."

"Ma'am, I mean no disrespect, but this is Texas. It's a whole different world down here than in Boston. Here folks tend to shoot first and ask questions later. Or in this case, hang first. You'd best just step back and let this old pro do his job."

"Can you keep him from—" She couldn't bring herself to say the word.

"From hanging? I don't know. I'll do my best."

He didn't know. Well, that wasn't good enough. But it would have to be good enough, considering she hadn't seen any other law offices around. She rose and held out her hand. "Thank you, Mr. Herrington. I'll consider your offer of help. I'm afraid I'll need some time to think about it, and I'll get back with you."

Herrington looked as if she could knock him over with her handkerchief. *My missing handkerchief*, she thought wryly, and then marveled at the odd paths her mind could take. "Good day to you," she called over her shoulder, over the jangling bell as she pushed open the door.

After being in that smoky office, even the Houston air seemed fresh. She breathed deeply and tried to still the storm inside her. But it wouldn't be stilled, and she felt a fresh flood of tears welling up. Turning to the right, she let her feet lead the way, faster and faster, back toward the hotel, until finally she ran. At least this time, she remembered the way. She ran right through the lobby and right up the stairs. Ran as fast as she could to her room, where she fumbled with her key, pushed open the door, threw herself on the bed and sobbed. For the first time since that awful moment just—was it just two hours ago?—when Evan was arrested, she let her emotions loose.

Had it really been just this morning that they'd argued over when to eat breakfast? She stuffed her face into her pillow and let out a groan that came from someplace deep within her. She could remember crying like this only once before, and that was when she'd returned home from her auxiliary meeting to find the doctor's carriage in front of her house. Geoffrey's face flashed through her mind, the sadness and pity she read there as he told her, in his quiet way, that her papa was gone. Geoffrey, ever the faithful servant.

The old butler had followed her up the stairs that day, waiting quietly as she knelt by Papa's bed, caressed his cold hand and begged him to wake up. Then he'd taken her gently by the shoulders as the doctor pulled the sheet up over Papa's head. Sweet Geoffrey. He'd pulled a chair by her door and sat there all night, interrupting her sobs from time to time to offer a glass of water or a bite to eat.

Well, Geoffrey wasn't here now, and Evan was in jail. *Dear God, will they really hang him? Please. I can't lose him, too. He's all I have left.*

After a time, she wasn't sure how long, she pulled herself to a seated position. She had to get hold of herself if she was going to be any help to Evan. The door to his suite was cracked open, and she decided to look through his things once again. Perhaps she'd missed something that could help him.

Draped over the back of a chair were the clothes he'd worn the day before. She lifted the pants and felt around in his pockets. Nothing. Of course, he would have emptied yesterday's contents and placed them in today's pair.

As she held the britches in front of her, she couldn't help but smile at their length. They were a perfect fit for her—lengthwise, anyway. Once, a few years back, she'd tried on his pants just for fun and had modeled them for Evan. Papa nearly had a conniption fit when he walked into the library and saw her!

If only she could— Wait a minute. Why couldn't she?

Within minutes a flurry of petticoats and lace lay in a heap on the floor, and Elizabeth examined her reflection in the full-length mirror. Not bad. She'd need a new shirt and overcoat; Evan's shoulders were broader than hers, while the buttons pulled at her chest. But the pants were fine once she'd used a hatpin to create a new hole in his belt and cinched it tight.

Somewhere in her bag was a pair of scissors. Back in her own room, she pulled everything out of her case in a mad search. There! Seating herself at the vanity with calculated determination, she pulled the pins from her dark hair one by one and set them aside. Dark waves spilled onto her shoulders and down her back, and she smoothed them with the brush, just as she tried to smooth down the anxiety in her stomach. It was only hair. It would grow back. A small price to pay to save Evan's life.

The deep breath was supposed to give her courage, but it didn't. She clenched her jaw, gathered a clump of hair in her left hand, and fit the scissor holes between her right thumb and forefinger. It was now or never.

Chapter 3

Water sloshed in the tin cup, and a few drops spilled as Rett handed it through the bars to his prisoner.

"Thank you," Hardy said and drained the contents in one long swig before offering the cup back to Rett.

"Your sister is determined to get you out of here," Rett told him. They both knew the woman who called herself Elizabeth Covington wasn't Hardy's sister, but Rett figured he might as well play along and see if Hardy offered any information about her.

"If there's any word that describes Elizabeth, it's *determined*." Hardy lowered himself to the bunk and leaned forward, resting his hands on his knees. "I'd like to speak with her, if that's all right."

Rett shifted his weight onto the other boot. "You have a right to an attorney, Mr. Hardy. But since she's obviously not your attorney, we can't let you meet with her privately. I suppose I might be able to arrange a short, supervised visit, but you'll have to stay behind those bars."

Hardy looked grateful. "That would be most appreciated. I'm worried about her. She's quite capable, but she's never been alone in a large, unfamiliar city."

What was his game? He hardly seemed the monster he'd been made out to be. Maybe Hardy had fallen for the girl. A pretty face could do crazy things to a man. It could even bring out the soft side in someone like James Weston Hardy.

If that was the case, perhaps Elizabeth Covington could play a vital role in wrenching some confessions from the man. It was rumored he'd killed over forty people, but only a couple dozen of those had been proven. A confession from Hardy could close a lot of case files and bring some measure of relief for many of his victims' families.

"I'm not sure where she is at the moment," Rett told him. "When she left a while ago, she planned to visit the lawyer down the street. She's not returned, but I'm sure she'll be back before long."

Hardy swung his legs onto the bunk and lay back against the flat pillow, his hands under his head. "I'm not him, you know."

"Who? Hardy? Yes, you've told me. Unfortunately for you, I think you are Hardy. And so does Sheriff Goodman, and so do the other half-dozen lawmen who've been in and out of here in the past hour."

"How can I prove to you that I'm not James Weston Hardy?"

Rett couldn't help but grin. This was entertaining. "Well, sir, if you're telling the truth, I'm afraid you're in a heap o' trouble. I guess only the real James Weston Hardy can prove your innocence."

The man on the bunk let out a heavy breath. "I was afraid of that."

A long, low creak sounded as Rett pushed from the old chair and placed his hat on his head. He needed to get out of here. Shoot. Even he was starting to believe this guy, which was absurd. No doubt about it. James Weston Hardy was either one of the most manipulative liars Rett had ever known, or...

Or this guy was telling the truth.

No, he was definitely a liar and a murderer. Of course he was manipulative. "Might as well make yourself comfortable, Mr. Hardy. I have a feeling you're going to be here awhile."

Cody and Ray were in the office area studying Hardy's profile. When they saw Rett, they both whistled and applauded, then reached to shake his hand. "So you really did it! You brought down James Weston Hardy. Not bad for a wet-behind-the-ears newcomer," Ray said. "I told Cody he was wrong about you."

All three laughed. "I wish I could say it was a big deal, but it really wasn't," Rett admitted. "Some guy recognized him from the flyer and pointed him out. He didn't fight at all when I arrested him."

Cody's jaw dropped. "Really? No struggle at all?"

"Nothing."

"Wow. That's surprising. How many lawmen has he killed?" Ray asked.

"I dunno. A lot." Rett pushed down the nagging feeling that something wasn't right. "He had a woman with him."

The other men laughed. "Now, that sounds more like Hardy. Where is she now? Is she a looker?"

If Rett hadn't known these fellows, he'd have never guessed they were two of the best lawmen in Texas. They could also be a couple of clowns. "She claims to be his sister. She's gone to secure him an attorney."

Ray referred to the file. "Which sister? Mavis or Nita?"

"Elizabeth."

Cody let out a low whistle. "New sister. Interesting."

"I'm expecting her back anytime now. As a matter of fact, she's been gone longer than necessary. Maybe I ought to go check on her."

Ray grinned. "So she is a looker."

"Be quiet, Ray." Rett couldn't help but grin at his mentor's ribbing. He knew he'd probably get it for a while, for no other reason than being the youngest man on the force. And for bringing in the most notorious criminal they'd seen in a long, long time.

Elizabeth set the scissors back on the vanity, her hair still intact. The sheriff had said he still needed to question her. If she disappeared, it would make Evan look guilty. And if she showed up as herself with short hair, they'd suspect something.

No. Best keep her hair long. She'd have to figure out some way to hide it. Using her comb, she parted it on the side and pulled it tightly to the nape of her neck. Perhaps if she folded her collar up just a bit… Yes, that could work.

It wouldn't be a problem at all, as long as she wore a hat. But she knew there would come a time when she'd have to remove her hat, and she needed to look the part at all times. A picture of the worker at the dock flashed through her memory. He'd had long hair. So had a few other men she'd encountered here in Texas. But each one had also sported a beard.

If she pulled her hair back, lowered her voice and spoke like a native Texan, perhaps everyone would just see her as eccentric. An eccentric man.

It could work.

She studied her face in the mirror. Her mother's face, so they told her. She studied, not for the first time, the smooth skin, the soft lines. Reaching up to touch her cheek, she noticed her hands. They were a woman's hands.

No one would buy it. Why, she was a fool for even considering such a preposterous idea. But she had to help Evan. Her heart raced again as she realized she was out of options. Stanley Herrington was her only choice.

Inhaling deeply, slowly, she willed herself to calm down. This could work. Herrington would just have to accept her help, whether he wanted it or not. She decided right then to hire the man. Today.

But first she needed to do some shopping. And some research.

Ten minutes later, she entered the general store across from her hotel. "I need to purchase some paper and pencils, please. And some postage stamps, if you have them."

The clerk nodded. "Yes, ma'am. Wait here, and I'll get them for you."

Elizabeth browsed the shelves while she waited and wondered what she might be forgetting.

Shoes! She was so tired of the proper-looking, ill-fitting ladies' boots she'd been forced to wear all her adult life. If she was going to do the work to prove Evan's true identity, she'd need more comfortable shoes. She eyed the work boots, but no. She had to maintain a modicum of dignity if she was to be taken seriously.

On the bottom shelf, she found a small pair of brown Western boots, the kind she'd seen cowboys wear. They were probably made for a boy, but they were simple. Not ostentatious or showy. And they looked comfortable.

Why, with her full skirts, no one would ever see. If Evan were here, he'd certainly advise against it. But surely he wouldn't object under the circumstances. She picked them up and carried them to the counter.

She added a few lace-edged handkerchiefs to the pile and opened her reticule. A familiar, unpleasant tobacco stench wafted her way moments before she heard Stanley Herrington's voice.

"Well, well, Miss Covington. Fancy seeing you here." The man looked at the boots, then at the paper and pencils the clerk placed beside them. A few wrinkles appeared on his vast forehead, but he said nothing more.

"Mr. Herrington. So good to see you again." Elizabeth searched her mind for what to say. "I've made a decision regarding the conversation we had earlier."

"Is that so?"

"Yes, sir. I've decided to allow you to represent Evan."

The man's eyes swung to the pile on the counter, then back at her. "So you agree to my condition?"

"I agree not to do anything that would hurt Evan's chances of going free."

Herrington harrumphed. "That's what I was afraid of." He looked again at the paper and pencils and shook his head. "Meet me in my office at four-thirty—not a minute later. I'll stop by the jail this afternoon and speak to your brother."

"Thank you," she whispered, then paid the clerk for her purchases. First thing, she planned to return to her hotel room and change into her new boots. Then she'd mill about town, ask a few questions. Perhaps someone could tell her more about this Hardy fellow.

A conversation behind her perked her ears. What was being said?

"Yes, that's right. James Weston Hardy was arrested!"

"You don't say. He put up a fight?"

"No. Not at all. Strange, given his background."

"Aw, I dunno. He probably knew he was beat."

"Mebbe so."

Elizabeth searched the crowded store for the source of the voices. One belonged to an elderly gentleman. The other came from a tall, dignified-looking man, perhaps in his late twenties or early thirties. Gossips, all of them. Men were just as bad as women.

Disgusted, she turned on her heel and made her way to the exit. As she pushed open the door, she collided with a wide expanse of chest wearing a five-pointed star pinned to the left side.

"Miss Covington! I was just coming to find you."

"Mr. Smith. I mean Ranger Smith. I'm sorry, but I'm not sure how to properly address you." Why did he seem amused? The cleft in his chin briefly caught her attention. *First his eyes, now his chin. Get hold of yourself, girl.*

"Rett is fine. We don't stand on ceremony around here."

The nerve! Who did he think he was? Of course she wasn't going to be on a first-name basis with the man who'd arrested Evan. Besides, she'd just met the man.

He must have sensed her disapproval, for he added, "Or Ranger Smith. Whichever strikes your fancy."

A slight nod of her chin delivered what she hoped was an aloof superiority. She needed to put this man in his place, knock that confidence down a notch or two. But she couldn't be too obvious about it. She didn't want to make an enemy. She just wanted to make him question his decision to arrest Evan.

"What can I do for you, Ranger Smith?"

He removed his hat. "Well, ma'am, I was concerned about you."

Yes. Of course you were, you big bully. "Oh? And why is that?"

"A woman as pretty as yourself, all alone in a big city. I just thought I could take you to lunch or something."

Was he flirting with her? Surely not. "I...um..." Drat! He'd caught her off guard. And why was he smiling at her that way? Of all the conceited, smug—

"And I have a few more questions about the man you call your brother and how the two of you became acquainted."

"That's a ridiculous question. We became acquainted the same way most siblings become acquainted. We shared parents, a home, a life."

A woman squeezed past them on her way into the

general store, and they both moved to a less crowded place on the sidewalk.

"I see. Well, I'm famished. And since I take the blame for interrupting your breakfast, I'd like to make it up to you. And ask you a few more questions, if you don't mind."

You think you're so charming, don't you? Well, Mr. Charm. You don't have me fooled. If you think I'm going to share a meal with you— Wait. What was it Papa had taught her? Keep your friends close and your enemies closer. Yes, that was it. Who'd said that? Sun Tzu, or something like that. An ancient Chinese military strategist.

Well, this was war. And this man was definitely the enemy, considering he was out to hang her brother. She smiled and tried to don a pleasant facade. "Why, thank you, Ranger Smith. I'd be honored."

"The honor is all mine, Miss Covington. If you'd like, we can stop by the jail. I can't allow an unsupervised visit, but I don't see what it would hurt to let you say hello."

Elizabeth felt the breath lunge from her chest, as if she'd been holding it since Evan's arrest earlier in the day. "Really? You'll let me see Evan?" Tears threatened again, disproving the notion she'd cried herself dry back in the hotel room.

He nodded. She wanted to hug someone. Truly, she might have hugged Ranger Smith despite her abhorrence of him if she hadn't known the truth of the matter. Somehow he was using her to prove his case. If he really believed Evan was this Hardy man, he surely hoped they'd slip up in communication and he'd overhear. Well, he wouldn't learn a thing. He could listen all he wanted. He couldn't prove something that wasn't true, could he? Starting tomorrow morning, she'd see to it that Evan had the best legal defense the big state of Texas had ever seen.

"Thank you, Ranger Smith." She took the elbow he offered and allowed him to lead her through town, to her brother.

Rett sat behind the small desk and pretended to read the newspaper while his ears tuned in to the conversation between Hardy and Elizabeth.

"Did you secure an attorney?"

Long pause. "Yes. Yes, I did."

"What's your impression of him?"

Elizabeth looked over her shoulder at Rett, but he didn't acknowledge her. She faced Hardy again and whispered, "The best I could find."

"When will I meet him?"

"He said he'd stop by later today. And I need you to promise me something."

"What's that?"

She lowered her voice again, and Rett turned his ear toward her, careful to keep his eyes on the paper. "No matter what you think, I want you to promise to give this lawyer a fair chance."

For several long moments, the only sounds in the room were the slight crinkling of Rett's paper and the beating of his heart. Finally, he saw Hardy nod. "I don't suppose I have much of a choice."

Elizabeth cleared her throat, and the conversation moved to other things. She asked if Hardy had eaten, if he was comfortable enough, if he needed anything from the hotel.

"Just take care of yourself. And get me out of here."

She reached through the bars to take Hardy's hand, and immediately Rett was on his feet. "I'm sorry, ma'am. You're not allowed to do that."

The look she sent Rett carried the whip of a scorpion's sting. How she managed that without speaking made Rett wonder what she was capable of. She withdrew her hand and touched it to her lips, then extended it toward Hardy. Man. She must have fallen hard for this guy.

Yet she didn't seem like a woman in love. Just… as though she cared deeply for the man behind bars. The whole thing was downright strange. What was that saying? "Truth is always stranger than fiction." Yes, indeed.

He touched her back. "Are you ready, Miss Covington? I'm afraid your time is up."

"Your lawyer will be here shortly, Evan. It's going to be all right. I promise," she tried to reassure him.

Hardy sat on his bunk. Somehow he didn't look convinced.

Rett gently guided her into the office, where Cody and Ray pretended not to look. When he brought her through the first time, you'd have thought they'd never seen a woman before. Didn't they have something better to do?

He led her past them but paused when they both coughed and cleared their throats. What? Now they wanted an introduction?

"Uh, Miss Covington. I'd like you to meet two of my fellow Rangers, Cody Wilson and Ray Davis."

Her smile was sweet, but there was an icy-hot fire in her eyes. "I wish I could say I'm pleased to meet you, gentlemen. However, considering your partner here is responsible for keeping an innocent man behind bars, I'm afraid I'm not pleased at all."

Cody coughed. Ray looked at his feet. After a moment, Cody said, "Well, ma'am. I hope everything works out for you."

She stood to her full height, confidence pouring out of her. "It will. If I have anything to do with it, my brother will be out of here in no time. And I'm a woman who is accustomed to getting her way."

The other two men just nodded, and Rett steered her once again to the door. "I thought we could eat at Market Square again, unless you have another preference."

"It makes no difference to me, Ranger Smith. I'm not a picky eater. I can eat just about anything. I would, however, like to see you eat a certain type of bird before my visit in Houston is complete."

He couldn't help but laugh at this spitfire, though he knew his chuckle would only add fuel to her flame. He had no intention of giving her that pleasure.

Chapter 4

Why had she agreed to share a meal with this man? And why did he have to be so suave? Honestly, Rett Smith was a perfect gentleman. He pulled out her chair for her. He made sure she was comfortable and had the best seat. He asked about her food, and when her water glass was nearly drained, he asked the waiter to bring her more. He spoke to her as though what she had to say was important. Not like so many men who spoke *at* her as if she were a child.

And every single nice thing he did made her like him even less. Why, what did he think she was? An idiot? Did he really think he could win some kind of confession from her just by trifling with her emotions?

Okay. He wasn't exactly flirting. But his polished manners grated on her nerves, probably because under different circumstances, she would have really liked this man. Liked to spend time with him. And the last thing in this world she wanted to do was be attracted to him. Why couldn't he match the stereotype she had of cowboys? Unwashed. Unrefined. Smelly. Why did he have to be so handsome and smell so nice?

Blast that man.

Guilt washed over her for entertaining such thoughts while Evan sat imprisoned. Evan! Her shoulders tensed, and the well-prepared meal turned to a mound of red ants in her stomach, stinging and burning from the inside out. Was he really being held for murder?

"Would you care for some dessert, ma'am?" the waiter asked, and Rett deferred to her.

"No, thank you," she replied coolly. Her tone sounded hostile even to her ears, and she knew she wasn't helping her cause or Evan's. *Get hold of yourself!* Her napkin fell from her lap, and Rett leaned over to retrieve it. She took the opportunity to breathe deeply and wipe the sour look from her face.

"The meal was delicious. Thank you," she told him when he was settled back in his chair. She hoped she sounded a bit more sociable.

"The pleasure was all mine, Miss Covington. I'm sorry for the circumstances, though."

"Then let my brother out of that horrid place!"

Rett set aside his own napkin and leaned back. "I'm afraid that's not going to happen, Miss Covington." He paused, as if weighing his next words. "Look, I usually have a pretty good sense about people. You seem like a good sort. I'm not sure how you got tangled up with Hardy, but the sooner you realize he's no good, the better off you'll be." He leaned forward, pressed his palms on the table and lowered his voice. "You're not the first person he's duped. If you'll come clean and tell me how you came to be involved with him, things will go better for you. By cooperating with the authorities, you'll save yourself a lot of trouble in the long run."

Why, the nerve of that man! Elizabeth took a moment to calm her galloping pulse, but it wouldn't obey her orders. Heat flushed through her chest, her neck, her ears, her face, even her scalp, as righteous indignation fought with her temper. When she felt she could speak in a calm voice, she took a deep breath. "No, you look. You say you have a good sense about people. Why don't you go spend some time with my brother? He's not Hardy. He's a good, kind, decent man. Why, since our father died, he's done everything in his power to care for me, to comfort me. He's the only family I have left. But that's not why I want you to free him. I'm asking you—" she paused, then lowered her voice to the softest whisper "—I'm begging you. Just consider the evidence. I saw the flyer. I know Evan looks like the image there. But consider the possibility that you're mistaken." Her napkin was now a twisted mess, and she forced her hands to relax. "Please," she added.

Rett remained as he was, leaning forward, and continued to study her for a moment. Finally, he gave the slightest nod. "I assure you, Miss Covington, I have no desire to convict an innocent man, and neither does anyone else. I'll do everything in my power to make sure your brother receives a fair trial."

That would have to do, she supposed. "Ranger Smith, I do thank you for the meal, but I really must be going." She pushed back her chair and placed the napkin on the table. "Unless, of course, you'd like to assist me in my attempt to free my brother."

"What type of assistance would you like?"

A wry smile touched the corner of her mouth. "Your keys would be a good place to start."

He laughed really loud at that, and several people turned to look. "I'm sorry, Miss Covington. But I find your wit to be…charming."

"I wasn't trying to be funny. But since you obviously won't help free Evan, I must be going." Elizabeth spun around, not caring that she created a scene that had captured the interest of several fellow diners. With shoulders squared and chin high, she marched through the restaurant, leaving the Ranger in her wake.

The swinging double doors opened a little more easily than she expected, and one of them banged against the outer wall of the restaurant. The fresh air on her face was a welcome relief, and she consciously slowed her gait. She had to get hold of herself. She needed paper and pencil— Her packages! She'd left them at the table, on the empty chair. Oh, mercy. Did she have to go back there, after the stir she'd caused?

"Miss Covington! You forgot these."

There was that blasted Ranger again, being all gentlemanly. She took the packages, and with a curt nod muttered her thanks, turned her back on him and headed toward her hotel. She needed to clear her head.

Rett watched Elizabeth Covington walk away and tried not to notice the pert sway of her skirts, the gentle curves of her back and waist. In his line of work, he saw a lot of raunchy men. Even saw some overdone, underdressed women. But to see a truly beautiful woman, one who was refined and cultured and ladylike, was a rarity.

Some might say she was too tall to be called a classic beauty, too bold and forthright to be called a true lady. But as far as he was concerned, Elizabeth Covington had all the right stuff. If he'd met her under different circumstances, he'd be following her instead of standing here on the sidewalk, trying to figure her out.

Apparently, Hardy thought Elizabeth was something, too. Rett couldn't get past the notion that Elizabeth seemed too intelligent, too sharp to be taken in by the likes of Hardy. Yes, he knew Hardy's profile. Well-spoken, well educated. A gentleman. It would be one thing if he'd lied to her and she knew nothing of his background.

But to get her to lie for him? Which was exactly what she was doing. Even if her name really was Elizabeth Covington, she'd lied about Hardy's name. Lied about her relationship with him.

Now all he had to figure out was, why? What was in it for her? Judging from the way she dressed, she seemed to appreciate fine things. Perhaps they'd planned a bank heist or a stage robbery. Something like that. And he'd promised her a cut of the money.

Or maybe Hardy had wooed her and won her, then convinced her to lie for him out of loyalty. Some women fell easy prey to controlling men like Hardy. But Elizabeth didn't seem the type to be bullied by a man.

No. He didn't believe for a minute she was being manipulated by Hardy. She simply didn't fit the profile of a lackey. If anything, she seemed the more forceful personality of the two.

Well, at least he knew where she was staying. Maybe he'd camp out across the street from her hotel in the tavern tonight, just to make sure she didn't try to bolt. He stood there on the sidewalk and watched Elizabeth longer than he needed to. Even with the midday crowd of workmen, delivering boxes and crates to and from the dock and local businesses, her height made her easy to spot. Finally, she disappeared around the corner, and he turned back toward the sheriff's office.

"Ranger Smith. I just saw your man," Stanley Herrington called out as Rett neared the office.

"Yes, I heard you were representing him. Did you get what you needed from Hardy?"

"You mean Mr. Covington."

Rett didn't respond.

"You know, Ranger Smith, you've no proof you've got the right man, other than a fuzzy flyer. Why, I've seen that flyer. I know a half-dozen men who could be mistaken for the shape on that page."

Rett took off his hat and held open the office door. No use arguing with a man who argued for a living. No matter. Herrington could argue till he was blue, which, considering the man's wheezing and puffing, wouldn't take much. There was no way they were letting James Weston Hardy walk out of this jailhouse, unless it was on his way to his own hanging. "Good day, Mr. Herrington. Let me know if the Rangers can assist you in your case."

Herrington laughed. "I'll do that."

Cody and Ray were still at the office; normally they'd be patrolling the area. Rett smiled. Even seasoned Rangers like those two got excited over a big arrest like Hardy.

"How was your rendezvous?" Cody teased.

Rett tried to think of a clever retort but thought better of it. Cody was the sharp-tongued, witty one of the bunch. Rett had learned his lesson more than once, trying to one-up the other Ranger. Best to just keep his mouth shut and grin as if he had a secret. Yeah, that was it. His silence would drive the other guys crazy.

"He eaten anything yet?" Rett asked as he unlocked the door to the jail section.

"Nope. Said he wasn't hungry. We gave him some water, though."

Rett closed the door behind him. Hardy sat on his bunk, elbows on his knees, his head in his hands. He looked up as Rett approached, and his hair stood on end from where he'd run his fingers through it.

"You really should eat something," Rett told him.

Hardy studied Rett for a moment before he spoke. "You seem like a nice fellow."

"I try to be."

"You seem the type to want to do the right thing."

Rett said nothing.

"I'm not Hardy."

"If that's true, I'm sure it will all come out in court."

"Will it?"

Again, Rett didn't answer. He didn't believe for a minute they had the wrong guy. But he did believe in the integrity of the justice system. He had to believe in it, or he couldn't defend it the way he was called as a Ranger to do. After a time, he leaned against the desk and offered a response. "I sure hope so."

Hardy nodded. "Me, too."

"I'll bring you a plate," Rett told him and headed for

the door. Even if he refused to eat, at least he'd have it. Maybe if he smelled food, he'd change his mind.

Ray's feet were propped on the front desk, his hat tilted over his face. "That you, Smith?" he mumbled.

"Yeah."

"Where's the girl?"

"Back at her hotel. She's a tough one. Didn't crack a bit."

"You losin' your touch with the girls, Smith?"

Cody guffawed. "How can he lose somethin' he never had?" He ducked when Rett wadded up one of Hardy's flyers and threw it at him.

"You're mistaking me for you, Cody. The women love me," Rett shot back, then remembered his private vow to keep quiet.

Ray lifted his hat just enough so his eyes showed. Just barely. "Don't you think somebody ought to watch her? What's her name again?"

"Elizabeth. And yes, I'm planning on taking the night shift, across from her hotel at the saloon."

"She stayin' at the Houston?"

"Yeah."

"Cody, make yourself useful. Go on over there and watch for her."

Cody looked as if he'd just been handed a big slice of birthday cake. "My pleasure."

"Rett, go home. Take a nap. I'll see you back here at sunset."

Rett didn't want to go home, and he didn't want Cody watching Elizabeth. But he knew better than to argue with Ray. Though he was only a few years older than Rett, Ray was the senior member of their team. While most of their work was done alone, they did have to answer to the senior Rangers. And if he was going to be up all night, and who knew how long into tomorrow, Rett really did need to rest up. Or at least try.

"All right." Cody grinned like the Cheshire cat from that nonsense book written by that British fellow— what was his name? Carroll. Lewis Carroll. Rett's ma had borrowed *Alice's Adventures in Wonderland* from a peddler who passed through their area about twice a year and had read it to Lisa and Eldon. Rett was going on sixteen at the time and had pretended not to listen.

Well, Cody could grin all he wanted as long as he didn't let Elizabeth escape. Rett couldn't help but wonder, though, if Elizabeth was the Alice of this story, or if she'd turn out to be the wicked Queen of Hearts.

Elizabeth tried to still her shaking hands as she wrote—scrawled was more like it—a list of questions about Hardy. The more she knew about Hardy, the easier it would be to prove Evan wasn't him.

Why couldn't she calm down? Since the arrest, thoughts had shot through her mind in rapid succession, and she couldn't seem to get hold of herself long enough to make sense of it all. She was normally calm and collected, but this whole day had her reeling. She felt so alone. So helpless. And helpless was not a feeling she was accustomed to.

Okay. She needed to learn where Hardy was from. His likes and dislikes. Perhaps details about his crimes. Where, exactly, he was last seen. Family? Yes, if he was from around here, perhaps he had family she could question. Yes! If she could get a family member of his to testify that Evan wasn't the true Hardy, that would be proof!

Then again, if Evan hanged, Hardy could go free. Why would a member of his family want to help her?

The pencil scraped against her finger, and she loosened her grip. Teeth marks. She hadn't realized she'd been biting the pencil, but now it wasn't comfortable to hold. Unclenching her jaw, she realized anew just how tense she was.

Papa would advise me to pray. Of course, that was what she should do, but she'd never put as much stock in prayer as her father had. Oh, she believed in God. Trusted Him, even. But she trusted herself more. She wasn't keen on waiting, and with God, one almost always had to wait.

No, all too often she'd been guilty of praying the obligatory prayer, then doing exactly what she felt was needed. And so things had almost always worked out for the best. But of course, up to now she'd always had her father or Evan to talk things over with, to ask for advice. Or to pull her out of any binds.

This time, she had only herself.

And God, she supposed.

"Well, Papa, you always told me that when I got to the end of myself, I'd find God. You told me when I didn't know what to do, ask God. There was a Scripture, wasn't there? In the book of James, I think. I can hear you quoting it now. 'If any of you lack wisdom, let him ask of God, that giveth to all men liberally.'"

She set aside her chewed-up pencil and moved across the room to the bay window overlooking the city street. Tucking one foot under her, she let the other foot dangle from the comfy cushioned bench and leaned back against the frame.

Below her, a team of horses pulled a wagon filled with who knew what, headed to who knew where. The driver adjusted his hat, then slapped on the reins, and the horses picked up their pace. People milled on the sidewalks across the street. A woman and child looked in the window of a candy shop. A man leaned against a post, chewing on a cigar. Funny how life just went on for them, though her world had slammed to a halt.

Her fingertips left prints on the previously spotless glass, and she felt bad that someone would have to clean up after her. Another thing Papa had taught her: don't feel entitled to have others serve you. Appreciate the staff's hard work, and don't create more work for them than necessary. She didn't know why that had been so important to Papa. Probably because he never had servants himself until he was grown.

She sighed and tried to stay focused on the task at hand. Praying. She needed to pray.

Okay, God. Here I am. And I don't know what to do.

She lay her head against the glass and closed her eyes. *Evan's in jail, Lord, being held for murder! They think he's some fellow named Hardy. But I suppose You already know that.*

Elizabeth brushed away another tear. See, this was what she didn't like about praying. Nearly every time she tried to pray sincerely, she ended up crying. And she didn't have time for tears. She got to her feet, marched back to the desk and gathered her pencil and list of questions. She'd have to talk to God later.

Chapter 5

Rett couldn't get comfortable. He'd gone straight to his boardinghouse, pulled down both shades in his room, kicked off his boots and crawled into bed. But try as he might, he couldn't force himself to sleep when his mind was spinning with the day's events.

Every Ranger dreamed of reeling in the big one, and it looked as if Rett had done it. And without really trying. In this case, the big one had simply fallen into his lap. Which, given Hardy's history, didn't make sense. Rett couldn't help but wonder about Hardy's motivations. And Elizabeth's, for that matter.

He turned onto his left side and tried to get comfortable. Was she resting in her room, as well? Or was Cody shadowing her, watching her every move? Rolling to his back, he reached up and fluffed his pillow, then repositioned it under his head. What could she possibly have planned? One look at her face, and he knew she wasn't going to walk away from this.

Which was what she should do. Surely a nice girl like Elizabeth Covington had family waiting for her somewhere. But no, she'd said Hardy was the only family she had left, hadn't she? Maybe that was it. She was alone and desperate, and Hardy played on her emotions. Now she was afraid of losing him, simply because she didn't have anyone else.

Yeah. That made more sense. Poor girl. Perhaps… maybe if he sat her down, filled her in on the extent of Hardy's crimes, she'd come to her senses. He hated to see someone as refined as Miss Covington throw away her future because she'd been conned.

He rolled over again, then gave up and sat up. Who was he kidding? He hated to see her throw her life away because she was the most intriguing woman he'd met in a long time. Ever.

Okay, he'd said it. Well, thought it, anyway. Acknowledged the highly unprofessional attraction he felt for the woman who more than likely aided and abetted one of the most ruthless killers of all time. And he had to get these feelings under control. Nip it in the bud, as his grandmother used to say.

Because if she figured out that she had any power over him whatsoever, she was likely to use that power to her advantage. To Hardy's advantage.

Yes, that was it. She was probably a common trollop, all dressed up.

But no. There was no way she could fake the refinement that rolled off her every word, her every move.

No. Her acting ability would not be his downfall. She would never be successful in manipulating him.

As long as he was aware of his Achilles' heel, he could protect it. Only this time, it wasn't his heel that needed protecting.

To an unsuspecting onlooker, Elizabeth looked like nothing more than a window-shopper, wandering aimlessly, examining shops and businesses along Houston's main street. At least, that was what she hoped she looked like. If she was going to find answers, she couldn't act as if she wanted answers. This was something else Papa had taught her. Don't throw questions at people as though you're throwing spears. Instead, gently prod the conversation along and display only a casual interest. Now, somewhere around here there had to be a place with…who? Old men playing checkers. Women whispering.

Gossipers.

Yet these Texans were as foreign to her as if she were traveling abroad. They weren't coy and polite like Bostonians. They seemed to say exactly what they thought, which was refreshing. It was one of the reasons she'd thought she might fit in well here.

That was, until all of this happened with Evan. Now all she wanted was to get her brother and get out of this godforsaken place as quick as she could. Which brought her right back to seeking information about Hardy. But she wasn't sure the gentle questioning technique would work here.

Shielding her eyes against the afternoon sun, she saw—there!—a newspaper office. There in big block letters it read The Houston Daily. A reporter! Why didn't she think of that before? A man was just leaving, locking the door behind him.

Her skirts bustled as she half walked, half ran across the street to catch him, nearly getting herself run over in the process.

"Excuse me, sir?" she called, and the man turned. He appeared to be in his early forties and wore a flat-billed newsboy cap and oxford-style shirt, open at the neck and rolled up at the sleeves. A stub of a pencil was propped behind his left ear, and he looked as if he hadn't shaved in a couple of days. He didn't look friendly, but he didn't look exactly unfriendly, either. More just…neutral. Curious.

"What can I do for you?" he asked.

"Um…" She stopped to catch her breath. "I…um…" Great. She'd finally found someone who might be able to tell her something about Hardy, and she sounded like an empty-headed fool.

"Look, lady. I'm on a deadline here, and I have to get to an interview. Maybe you can come back to-morrow?"

"Have you heard about the Hardy arrest?" she blurted out before he could walk away.

That got his attention. "Yeah. I sure have. You know something?"

"It's not him. They have the wrong man."

Why the man laughed, she wasn't really sure. She didn't see one bit of humor in it. But that man let out a loud guffaw that sounded both cynical and mean. When he finally stopped laughing long enough to look at her face, he straightened. "Oh, you're serious."

"Of course I'm serious. Why wouldn't I be?"

"I have no idea, lady. But after all the hustling I've done in the last few hours to get this story to press on time, it would be some kind of sorry joke to learn it's the wrong fella. For my own sake, I sure hope you're wrong."

"I'm not wrong. And if you'll give me just five minutes of your time, I'll prove it to you."

The man wiped sweat off his brow and looked past her. "Sorry, lady. I don't have five minutes. Right or wrong, this story's going to press. This is the biggest thing to hit our town since…well, ever. And I'm counting on it to sell papers."

"Even if the story is wrong? You're risking your reputation as a serious newspaper if you don't take the time to check your facts, sir."

"Look, lady. I've spent all day checking facts. If I'm wrong, it's not because I haven't done my homework. If they really do have the wrong guy, it's the Rangers who will look foolish, not me. And certainly not my paper." With a curt nod, he took off at full speed.

Gathering her skirts, she ran after the man, her new Western boots clomping on the wooden sidewalk. She'd almost forgotten she was wearing them—they were that comfortable. "Print your story if you must. But then, if you'll give me just a few minutes of your time, I can promise you a story that will sell twice as many papers as this story."

The man slowed, then stopped. "What did you say your name is?"

"I didn't. My name is Elizabeth Covington, and the man they have locked in the jail is my brother, Evan. Not James Weston Hardy."

He laughed again, only this time he sounded more confused than cynical. "Name's Larry. Larry Thomas, owner of the *Houston Daily*." He offered his hand.

She took it, squared her shoulders and looked him directly in the eye. "Pleased to meet you, Mr. Thomas."

"I'll tell you what, Miss Covington. If you'll meet me back at my office in, say, three hours, I'll listen to what you have to say. I'm afraid that's the best I can do for you right now."

"Thank you. I'll see you in three hours, then."

With that, Larry Thomas was off. She hurried away, only briefly pausing to look at a hat in the window of the millinery shop. Her gift for shopping and fashion was almost as pronounced as her gift for arguing, and she needed the momentary distraction. She allowed her gaze to travel past the hat and into the store, and what she saw there made her heart race like a train on a downhill slope.

Cody leaned against the outer wall of the ladies' hat shop when Rett passed by on his way to the saloon. "What are you doing over here? I thought you were tailing Miss Covington."

One corner of Cody's mouth lifted in a kind of half smile. Then he motioned with his head through the propped-open door.

Rett followed Cody's gaze. Standing in front of a mirror was Elizabeth, surrounded by several of the town's busybodies and a pile of hats. Had she tried on every hat in the store?

"I think this one suits your coloring," said Bonetta Lewison, the mayor's wife.

"Do you think?" asked Elizabeth, turning this way and that in front of the mirror. "I think it's more suited to your coloring." She took the hat off her head and placed it on the older woman's. "There. Just look how that brings out the blush in your cheeks!"

Mrs. Lewison smiled, then patted her hair. "I suppose it does look nice. I'll take it."

The women gibbered like a bunch of hens, and Rett sighed. If this was what the evening held, it was going to be a long night indeed. Then his ears perked up.

"How long ago did you say that Hardy man was spotted in the area? I mean, before today, of course."

"Oh, I'd say it was two or three weeks ago. That's why Mavis and I haven't been to town since then. We were afraid to set foot on Main Street, or anywhere else." This was from Pat Harris, the Methodist preacher's wife.

Mavis, who was married to the blacksmith, nodded. "That's right. I was so relieved when Ed came home after lunch to tell me Hardy had been captured."

Elizabeth tried on another hat and modeled it for the ladies. "What do you think about this one?"

The old ladies clicked and clucked and oohed and aahed, as if Elizabeth were a life-size doll and they were little girls dressing her up. "I haven't seen one that didn't suit you, dear," said Bonetta.

"It's odd that Hardy evaded the law for so many years, but he stuck around here even after he'd been spotted. It seems to me he would have hastened away from here at the first sign of trouble," Elizabeth said.

Pat laughed. "Yes, it seems any sensible man would have hustled out of here weeks ago. Then again, any man who kills as ruthlessly as Hardy doesn't have much sense, if you ask me."

"I heard he did leave," said Mavis, and the others turned to look at her. "Ed told me the day he was first spotted that he stopped by the shop, had his horse re-shoed and headed east."

"You never told me that," said Pat.

"Ed told me to keep quiet. The last thing we wanted was Hardy coming back after us because Ed blabbed where he was going."

The ladies nodded. Elizabeth picked up another hat, this time placing it on Mavis's head. "I think it suits you," she said.

Mavis examined herself in the mirror. Rett just shook his head. Elizabeth had these women eating out of her hand. Unfortunately for Elizabeth, they didn't have any real information for her. So Hardy had gone east. He came back.

Cody cleared his throat, pulling Rett's focus from Elizabeth. He'd almost forgotten Cody was there. "I thought you were catching some shut-eye."

"I tried. Couldn't sleep."

"Pretty exciting day, huh?"

"I guess you could say that." Rett scooted back and watched the ladies through the window, but he couldn't hear as well from that vantage point. He moved close to the door again.

"Well, if you're gonna stick around here, I think I'll go check out the saloon, see if there's any fights I can break up. I can feel my manhood seeping from me the longer I listen to all the hat talk. Why, a minute ago, I caught myself thinking the red one would look good on Mavis."

Rett snorted a little too loudly, then stepped back in case the ladies inside had heard him. "That's probably a good idea. I was thinking you looked a little less manly."

Cody sent him a warning look, then pushed away from the wall and headed for the saloon.

Elizabeth could barely contain the smile that fought to burst through or the pounding of her pulse as she exited the millinery shop. What had she just done? Oh, my word. She'd watched Papa and Evan question people for a case, but she'd never really done it for herself! Once, she'd struck up a conversation with her neighbor's nanny in order to gain information for one of Papa's clients, but she'd learned nothing new. And when her father found out she'd been snooping, he'd told her to stay out of it. *I won't have you putting yourself in danger because of me or a client. If I can't trust you to leave things alone, I'll stop discussing my cases with you.* She'd never tried that again.

"How d'you do, Miss Covington."

She found herself standing in a tall shadow. Rett! Was he following her? Her temper flared, even though she knew she shouldn't be surprised. Well, let them tail her or trail her or whatever they called it. She had the truth on her side and nothing to hide.

"Can I help you with something?" she asked.

"No, not a thing," Rett said, stepping in front of her. "On second thought, I've wanted to purchase a birthday gift for my little sister. Perhaps you can help me select a hat."

"I'm sure there are plenty of ladies in Houston who'd be more than happy to oblige you, Ranger Smith. I'm afraid I can't help you, though. I'm late for an appointment." She bit her lower lip, looked at the ground and berated herself for talking too much. She didn't owe him an explanation.

"I'm impressed, Miss Covington," said Rett. "You had those ladies behaving like trained poodles. They're not usually so hospitable. Why, some of those ladies can be brutal, especially with newcomers."

"That's ridiculous. Why, they were as sweet as could be." Elizabeth forced her chin up and her shoulders back and moved past him. "If there's nothing I can do for you, I must be on my way. As I said, I'm late for an appointment."

"With who?" he asked.

"With whom," she corrected. "And that's none of your business."

"I suppose that's true. But it won't keep me from following you."

"It's a free country, I suppose." She sped up.

Rett kept time with her. He didn't frighten her; she knew in her gut Rett was on the right side of the law. He was simply wrong. But that didn't keep him from annoying her to no end. Finally, she stopped, and Rett nearly stumbled over his own feet.

"Ranger Smith," she said. "Perhaps you can help me with something. I know I can come to you if I feel someone is harassing me."

Rett nodded, like a child eager to please his parent.

"Well, to whom do I report you, for harassing me?"

A grin threatened to break through Rett's serious facade, though she didn't see the humor. He removed his hat.

"I do apologize, ma'am. I suppose I am harassing you, though that was never my intent."

Elizabeth felt her jaw tighten. "I accept your apology on one condition."

"What's that, ma'am?" Rett asked, and though his

frown was in place, there was something about the way his eyes crinkled that made her think he was laughing at her. Well, no matter. She didn't have time for this.

"Leave me alone. I have work to do."

Rett nodded. "I understand. I'll do my best, Miss Covington."

Elizabeth had stopped rolling her eyes when she was a young teenager. Nanny Carolyn had drilled it into her head that it was unattractive, foolish and rude. But if she ever wanted to roll her eyes, it was now. This man was…was… Ugh! She couldn't even think straight. "Thank you." She clipped her words, then moved past him, only to realize she was headed in the wrong direction.

Well, she wasn't about to turn around now. She'd just circle around the block and approach Mr. Herrington's office from the other side. Cutting left through the alley, she held up her skirts and picked her way over some old boards and bricks. At the back side of the building, she turned left again.

Perhaps this wasn't such a good idea. Though she saw nothing to alarm her, something didn't feel right. The hairs on the back of her neck stood up, and she moved a little faster, grateful again for the practical boots. She was about halfway to the next alleyway when she heard a long, low growl from behind a trash can.

Jumping, she turned toward where the sound originated. Cloaked in shadows was the shape of a dog. All she could really see, though, were the whites of its eyes and a set of long, sharp bared teeth, poised for attack.

Chapter 6

"Easy, now," Elizabeth whispered, working to keep fear from her voice. She held one arm out in front of her, palm up, hoping the animal would respond to the don't-come-any-closer gesture. Her left boot landed on something behind her as she backed away, something wobbly, and she eased her foot down. Was it a board?

She was afraid to take her eyes from the dog; instead, she kept talking in what she hoped was a low, soothing tone. The animal continued to growl. It advanced slowly, tail low, and its upper lip quirked and snarled. She'd heard animals could smell fear, but she couldn't help but feel afraid. Her pulse felt like a cannon against her chest. Should she run? Stand firm? In the corner of her eye, she saw a pile of wooden crates. Perhaps if she climbed on top of them, she'd be safe. Assuming they didn't topple.

Using her peripheral vision, she guided herself toward that stack, then stepped up onto the first box. It seemed sturdy enough. Now up to the second one.

A piece of loose wood fell from the top of the pile and startled the dog, and he came at her. She turned and clawed her way toward the top, but all around her, boxes tumbled. One landed on the hem of her skirt, and when she tried to get loose, she couldn't. It was caught!

She did the only thing she knew to do: covered her head with her arms, bent into herself and waited for the attack. But instead of feeling teeth clawing into her flesh, she heard Rett's voice.

"Whoa, there!"

The angry barks seemed to turn in another direction, followed by a bang and a yelp. Had he shot the dog?

Peering through her fingers, she saw Rett standing in front of a large upside-down crate, one foot resting on top of it. Through the slats, she saw the black dog licking his paw and whining softly.

"You know, you really shouldn't be back here. It's not safe." Rett's eyes never left the dog, and something about his tone of voice told her he was annoyed.

Well, let him be annoyed. She hadn't asked him to rescue her. "Perhaps if you weren't following me, I wouldn't have felt the need to take this route. I was trying to escape."

His head swung around at that. "Really? Well, Miss Covington, I find that rather interesting. Perhaps we need to take you down to the jail and lock you up with your brother."

"You can't do that! I've done nothing wrong!"

"Just being associated with James Weston Hardy is crime enough. And you just admitted you were trying to escape."

"From you!" she yelled, exasperated. She was normally so levelheaded. Why did this man get under her skin?

"What?" He really looked confused. Could he truly be so dense?

Just then another box shifted beneath her, and she nearly lost her balance. She tried to stand, but her skirt was still caught. Great. One of her nicest traveling dresses, too. She tugged gently, then harder, until *riiiiiip*! She heard the fabric tearing. At last she was free of the heavy boxes.

"You're bleeding," Rett said.

Holding her hands and arms in front of her, she examined herself for cuts.

"Not there. Your leg. It's bleeding."

He had seen her leg! She turned away for modesty, then gently lifted the hem of her now-tattered skirt. Sure enough, blood trickled from her calf, just above the top of her boot. A rusty nail, no doubt. Dropping the skirt, she whirled around. "I'm fine. Just a little nick."

"You need to clean that up. It could get bad if you don't."

"I'll make sure it's properly treated." It dawned on her then that she could just walk away from him. He was stuck, his boot providing the only security against the nervous dog under the crate. "Thank you for your assistance, Ranger Smith."

"Wait!" He scanned the alley, then pointed to a pile of bricks to her right. "Could you hand me some of those?"

Oh, for heaven's sake. She wouldn't be in this mess if it weren't for him. She picked her way through the boards and grabbed two bricks, then picked her way back and handed them to him. "There."

"Thank you, but I'll need more."

"How many more?"

"The entire pile."

"Mr. Smith, I'm grateful for your help, but—" She paused. She really was obliged. Why, more than her dress would be in shreds if Rett hadn't intervened. And here she was acting anything but appreciative. Her eyes took in her surroundings once more, focused on the dog in the crate, then lifted to meet his gaze. "I really am grateful. Thank you for rescuing me."

For the briefest moment their eyes locked, and something passed between them. Some sort of connection or understanding… She wasn't sure how to describe it. But just as quickly he looked down at the dog and the moment was lost.

"Just doing my job, ma'am."

"Oh…yes. I suppose you were." Elizabeth picked her way back to the bricks and, two by two, handed them to Rett, who piled them on top of the crate. Then he lifted a long metal pipe that had rolled out from under some of the boxes and slid it through the slats in the dog's crate and connected it to two other crates, one on each side. Finally, he surrounded the crate with several heavier crates.

"This should hold him until I can get back. I need to show you where the doctor's office is."

"I told you I'll be fine, Ranger Smith. I have an appointment, and I'm extremely late."

"What kind of appointment?"

There went her hackles again. "I don't see how that's any of your business." With a flip of her head, she turned and marched out of the alley. It would have had a much nicer effect if she had actually marched, instead of stopping every few feet to climb over the mess she'd helped create.

Rett looked back at the caged dog, breathed a prayer that it would still be caged when he returned and followed Elizabeth out of the alley. "Miss Covington, wait."

She kept walking. But was that a limp? It was, though she looked to be trying very hard not to limp. "Miss Covington!"

He knew she heard him. His voice was pretty loud. Others on the street turned to look, but she just kept marching onward, like some kind of queen ignoring the peasants and half-wits. That was one stubborn woman.

All the way to Stanley Herrington's law office he followed her. The office was locked.

"Oh, dear," Elizabeth said, jiggling the door handle. "I just assumed he'd be here. How silly of me."

As if on cue, Stanley Herrington huffed around the corner. He stopped short when he saw Elizabeth and Rett. "Somebody throw a party and forget to invite me?" he asked.

"I was hoping I could speak with you privately, Mr. Herrington."

"Well, by all means. Let me by so I can unlock the door."

She stepped aside for the older man, and while he fumbled with his keys, Elizabeth leveled Rett with one of her looks. "Thank you for all your help, Ranger Smith, but I don't require further assistance from you. Good day."

He tipped his hat and turned to leave. Little did she know he planned to circle the block and plant himself in this very spot.

If only Elizabeth could convince this man that she was qualified to help in the case, she'd feel better.

"You think I can't handle things, Miss Covington?" the man harrumphed.

"No, sir. It's not that. But I—"

"I'll be glad to keep you informed about any new developments. But as I told you before, things are done differently here in the Lone Star State. You need to let me take care of this."

She didn't see that she had a choice. At least he was willing to discuss the case with her. The two conversed about details of the arrest and Hardy's recent whereabouts for more than an hour. Finally, she excused herself. Mr. Thomas didn't seem the type to wait if she was late.

Rett stood in the shadows across the street. This time, she was determined to lose the man. At least for a little while. She turned once again into the alley, then, thinking better of it, went back to the main walkway. Peering around the corner, she saw Rett conversing with that other Ranger. The tall one. Cody, she thought. Blast that man!

There. The candy store was still open, though the owner inside looked to be closing things up for the night. Maybe she could slip over there without Rett seeing.

"Good evening," the man said as she closed the door behind her. "We're about to close, but I still have a few things out. What can I get you?"

Elizabeth peered out the window. Rett was looking up and down the street. She watched him turn into the alley where she'd started off. Good. That should keep him busy. "I'll have…" She turned to study the items behind the glass display case. Licorice! Evan loved licorice. "I'll take three licorice sticks and one peppermint stick please," she told the man.

After counting out her coins and thanking the man, she hurried into the dusk. Great. Now she was five minutes late. A short time later, she stopped at the *Houston Daily* office and tried to open the door. It was locked.

Rett arrived at Elizabeth's side just in time to hear her let out a cross between a huff and a snort.

"Miss Covington." He spoke softly this time, leaning forward and bringing his face very close to hers.

"See there? I've missed my appointment, all because you wouldn't leave me alone. What do you want, Ranger Smith? You have my brother. What more could you possibly want from me?"

He straightened and tried to rein in his thoughts back from their wayward responses to that question. "I…I want to help you."

Her lips pressed together with a tightening of her

jaw, and he was glad in that moment that her eyes weren't loaded with real bullets. If they had been, he'd have been a goner. "No, you don't. You want to see my brother hanged. I hardly call that helping me."

Boy. She wasn't giving up on this charade. He took a step back. "Your leg, Miss Covington. We need to tend to your leg."

She ran a well-shaped feminine hand across her brow and pushed back a loose curl. He wished she wouldn't; that dark, shiny curl made her look young. Vulnerable. Part of him wanted to touch it, see if it felt as silky as it looked.

He needed to get his thoughts under control. Maybe Ma was right. Maybe he did need to find a wife, settle down. Then he wouldn't be looking at a stray accomplice as if she were the last piece of cherry pie at the buffet.

"I really needed to keep this appointment, Ranger Smith. If you'll point me in the direction of the clinic, I promise to see to my leg as soon as I'm done here. Better yet, I believe there's a physician's office next door to my hotel. I'll see him as soon as I return."

Rett looked at the door she'd just tried to open. "It doesn't look like anyone's here."

"I know. I'm probably too late. Still, I'd like to wait a little while, just in case he returns."

A familiar-looking young woman approached them, then stood back as if she wanted them to move. Where had he seen her before?

"Excuse me," the woman said. "Are you Elizabeth Covington?"

"Yes, I am."

The smaller woman held out her hand. "I'm Amelia Cooper. I work for Mr. Thomas. He's been detained, so he asked me to meet you here."

Elizabeth looked at the dainty woman in front of her and took her hand. Blond hair streaked with varying shades of brown swept back from a face Renoir would have loved to paint. Perfect features. Tiny waist. Enormous eyes and heart-shaped lips. She was everything Elizabeth wasn't.

"Pleased to meet you, Miss Cooper."

Something about the woman's firm handshake made Elizabeth believe that in spite of her daintiness, this was a woman to be reckoned with. She decided right away to make an ally of Amelia Cooper.

Amelia nodded to Rett and unlocked the door. "Mr. Thomas told me you have an exclusive for us. I'm excited to tell your story."

Rett cleared his throat, but Amelia ignored him. She held the door open for Elizabeth but let it shut behind her, leaving Rett to let himself in. When he did follow the ladies inside, Elizabeth felt she might scream.

She didn't have to.

"Oh, Ranger Smith, isn't it?" Amelia asked.

Rett nodded.

"I wasn't aware you were to be part of this interview." Amelia looked to Elizabeth for confirmation, and Elizabeth shook her head in the negative. "It's probably best if you let us have some privacy. I'll find you later for comment if I find the need." She retraced her steps to the door, opened it and smiled sweetly at Rett.

The Ranger looked stunned, and Elizabeth wanted to giggle. He replaced the hat he'd just removed, nodded and said, "Ladies." Then he left.

Just when Elizabeth thought she was free of him, he opened the door again. "Don't forget to have a doctor look at that cut." Then he really left, but he didn't go far. She and Amelia watched through the window as he walked across the street and leaned against a post. When he saw them watching, he smiled and waved.

Amelia laughed. "I'm sure he'd love to be a fly on the wall. Why don't you come with me? We can sit in Mr. Thomas's office in the back. That's where the comfortable chairs are."

"So you're a reporter? I'm impressed. You don't see too many female reporters," Elizabeth commented as she followed Amelia through the office.

"I guess you could say that. I've wanted to be a real reporter for ages, but Mr. Thomas usually limits me to articles about recipes and sewing."

"Oh…I see." Elizabeth felt her hopes plummeting once again. She didn't think they could plummet any lower. Obviously Mr. Thomas hadn't taken her seriously, or he'd have been here himself.

Amelia sat in one of the leather chairs and gestured for Elizabeth to sit in the other. "Were you really with Hardy when he was arrested?"

Where hope had dropped, anger rose. "He's not Hardy! That's what I'm trying to tell everyone. They have the wrong man. And no one will listen to me!"

Amelia's cupid lips lifted into a hint of a smile,

and she nodded once. "Very good, Miss Covington. That's what Mr. Thomas told me. I just wanted to see your reaction."

Elizabeth wasn't sure what to say, so she said nothing. If the day had gone as planned, Evan would be with her right now, and they'd be discussing whether to read books or play chess. Would she ever play chess against her brother again?

Of course she would. She had to keep pressing forward. He was innocent. Surely God wouldn't allow...

"Miss Covington, why don't you start by telling me what you and your brother are doing in Houston."

"Please, call me Elizabeth." She inhaled, then exhaled slowly and tried to calm her nerves. "Evan just graduated from law school, and—"

"Where?"

"Excuse me?"

"Where did he graduate from law school?"

"Oh, Harvard." Elizabeth watched Amelia jot that down, then continued, "Our father passed away last January, and we're still dealing with that loss. Evan thought it might be nice for us to take a trip together, get away from things, before he settled into his law practice."

"Does he already have a position with a firm?"

"He's had several offers, but he hasn't made a decision yet." Elizabeth paused while Amelia scrawled.

"Where is your home?" she asked.

"Boston. We traveled here by train and made many stops along the way. We're taking our time, getting a feel for different parts of the country. It's been fun...a nice reprieve from our grief."

"What other stops did you make before arriving in Houston?"

Elizabeth continued with her story, answering questions. The more she talked, the more comfortable she felt with Amelia.

Finally, Amelia asked, "Tell me, Elizabeth, what do you want readers to know? If you could say anything at all to our readers, what would it be?"

"They've arrested the wrong man."

"Can you prove it?"

"I sure hope so."

Neither of them said anything for a time, and the only sound from within the office was the tick-ticking of the grandfather clock in the next room. After a while Amelia broke the silence. "I believe you."

"You do?"

"Yes. And I'd like to help you. I'm not sure what I can do, but I'll do what I can."

That was all it took for the floodgates to open again. Elizabeth hated blubbering in front of someone she barely knew. Amelia passed her a handkerchief, and Elizabeth blew her nose with a very unladylike honk. "Thank you, Amelia."

"You're welcome. Thank you for telling me your story."

Again, there was an awkward silence. Amelia broke it again. "Just so you'll know, I'm pretty sure Mr. Thomas sent me to do this interview hoping I'd get you to work out an interview with your brother."

"What?"

"He doesn't think you're the big story. But an interview with Hardy—"

Elizabeth opened her mouth to speak, but Amelia held out her hand.

"I know he's not Hardy. As I said, I believe you. But Mr. Thomas is a different story. He just wants an exclusive."

"What if I get you the exclusive?" Elizabeth asked her new friend.

"Me?"

"Yes. What if I get Evan to agree to an interview, but only with you?"

Amelia smiled, then laughed out loud. "That would eat Mr. Thomas alive, I can tell you right now."

The two women locked eyes and smiled. "Let's do it," Elizabeth told her, and they shook hands before rising from their chairs. "When can we meet again?"

"How about first thing in the morning? But not here. I don't want Mr. Thomas to know about our plan until the wheels are already rolling."

"I know," said Elizabeth. "Why don't you meet me at my hotel for breakfast. Say, eight o'clock?"

"Sounds perfect."

They walked together to the front door, and Elizabeth couldn't resist looking out the window. "He's still there."

"Get used to him. I've watched the Rangers for years. When one of them is on a case, he thinks of little else."

"And I suppose I'm considered part of his case."

"Yep."

Elizabeth reached for the doorknob, but Amelia surprised her with a hug. "It's going to be all right, Elizabeth. I just have this feeling."

"I hope you're right." Elizabeth and Amelia went in opposite directions. Elizabeth decided there was one good point about being part of a Ranger's investigation. She didn't have to worry about being out after dark. She knew that, as annoying as he was, Rett wouldn't let anything happen to her.

She pretended she didn't know he followed her, and went straight to the physician's office next door to the hotel. She knew it was after hours, but Rett was right, much as she hated to admit it. Her leg was throbbing. She knocked three times and waited, hoping for an answer.

A few moments later, a disheveled-looking white-haired gentleman arrived. His tired eyes squinted against the lamplight in the room. "What can I do for you, ma'am?"

"Is the doctor available? I'm afraid I had a rather unfortunate run-in with a nail."

"I'm Dr. Herman. Come on in and show me what's ailing you."

Elizabeth followed the man down a short hallway into a small, well-ordered office and had a seat on the examination table. She lifted her skirt carefully so just the skin at the top of her boot showed.

"Oh, my. That's nasty looking. Wait right here, and I'll get you all fixed up." He disappeared into some sort of closet or storage room and returned with a brown bottle, some cotton and some bandages. Setting the items on his desk, he grabbed a pencil and handed it to her.

She looked around for some paper, wondering what he wanted her to write.

"Bite on it," he told her, but she just stared at the man. For the life of her, she couldn't figure out what he was saying.

"Bite on it," he said. "The pencil. This is going to sting pretty bad. It helps if you have something to bite on."

"Oh," she said and stuck the pencil between her teeth.

Chapter 7

A stifled groan seeped through the closed door, and Rett felt his shoulders tense with an odd combination of sympathy and relief. At least Elizabeth wouldn't wake up someday with lockjaw. He knew the doc cleaned the wound with carbolic acid, and it would probably keep her awake for a while unless she was also given something for pain. Yeah, Doc would probably give her some laudanum, too. She'd be fine if he did.

He heard a shuffle from inside, then Doc's soft voice, though he couldn't make out the words. The door opened, and Elizabeth hobbled into the hallway. Doc was right behind her.

"Rett! I didn't expect to see you here," Doc said. "Are you waiting for me?"

His eyes were on Doc, but Rett didn't miss the tears Elizabeth swiped with her hand as she headed toward the door. "No, sir. I just wanted to check on Miss Covington, here. I hope you don't mind I let myself in."

"Of course not. You're always welcome in my office. You two know each other?" Doc touched Elizabeth's retreating shoulder, and she turned.

"We've met. Ranger Smith was kind enough to rescue me from an attacking dog, which is why I slipped and, well…you know the rest. Thank you for your help, Doctor. Ranger Smith." Elizabeth offered Doc an appreciative smile but didn't give Rett more than a curt nod.

"I see," said Doc. "Ranger Smith is one of the finest young lawmen I know. By the way, Rett, everyone's talking about you."

"Is that so?" Rett shifted his weight. He had a feeling he knew where this conversation was headed.

"Yes. You're a big hero! Imagine. Capturing someone like Hardy, all by yourself. Good job!" It felt nice to hear the pride in the older man's voice. Doc had nursed Rett back to health after a bullet grazed his left thigh, right after he joined the Rangers. Not much damage, but it had been enough to frustrate a young Ranger to no end. He'd wanted to be out catching bad guys, but Doc had insisted there'd be plenty of time for that later. He was right. Over the past few months, Rett had learned there was never a shortage of miscreants and lawbreakers. Guys like Hardy, however, were rare.

Elizabeth tried to leave again, but Doc stopped her. "Don't forget—one packet of the laudanum with a glass of water or tea as soon as you get ready for bed. It will help you sleep. You can take some more in the morning if you're still in pain. Plan on staying in bed if you do, though. The stuff makes you pretty sleepy."

"Thank you, Doctor. I'll keep that in mind." This time, Elizabeth was successful in her attempt to escape the conversation. But it was Rett's job to make sure she didn't escape from Houston and take Hardy with her.

"Doc, it was nice seeing you." He hated to cut the man off, but he was on duty. "Miss Covington!" he called.

She kept walking, pain cinching her steps. "What do you want, Ranger Smith?"

"I just wanted to ask if you're okay. Carbolic acid can sting pretty bad." He followed her into the hotel lobby.

"I'm fine. I'd be better if you'd disappear, but so far my prayers in that direction haven't been answered." Her voice was thin, pinched, and he wished he could carry her up the stairs. He was all too familiar with the discomfort she must be feeling.

"Can I help you up the stairs?"

Her knuckles turned white as she gripped the railing at the bottom of the staircase, but he wasn't sure if it was from pain or annoyance. A moment passed as she considered his offer. "I suppose."

Ouch. Her pride must be hurting worse than her leg right now. Rett looked around, and other than the desk clerk, the lobby was deserted. It was too late for the dinner crowd, too early for those who were prone to certain types of mischief. Without asking permission, he scooped her into his arms and started up the steps.

"Ranger Smith, put me down this instant! What do you think you're doing?" Her words were strong, but her voice seemed weak, almost relieved. She laid her head on his shoulder even as she protested, and the warmth of her body next to his, the sweet, clean scent of her hair—what was that smell?—sent his thoughts reeling, not to mention his senses. He picked up his speed and set her down as soon as they reached the second-floor landing, but the effect of having her so close would stay with him well into the night.

Elizabeth didn't know what disturbed her more—the searing pain of her leg wound or the fact that she found Rett Smith's arms around her both unsettling and pleasant. What was she thinking?

She'd never been that close to a man, other than her father and Evan. And they certainly never stirred her feelings the way Rett's touch did. Oh, her traitorous heart! The excitement of being so close to a man—a tall, handsome man, at that—played tricks on her mind. That was all this was, just her misplaced longing for danger and adventure and…something else she didn't want to think about right now.

He set her down, and she backed away from him, breathless. She could still feel the warmth of his breath on her neck. Had she rested her head on his shoulder?

She had! Heat flooded her face and ears, and she knew if she looked in the mirror, she'd be red as a beet. Should she speak? Yes…but her lips had suddenly stopped working, as well as her mind. Instead, she made a pretense of smoothing her skirt, holding her head down so he wouldn't see the effect he had on her.

"Be sure to take that laudanum, like Doc said," Rett told her, but she still didn't look up. "He knows what he's talking about. It will take the pain away, and you'll sleep like a baby."

"I take it you've had experience with carbolic acid?" She couldn't think of what else to say. He should really just go.

"Yeah. Doc treated a leg wound for me."

An awkward silence fell between them, and she finally worked up the courage to look in his face. "Thank you for your help, Ranger Smith. I can take it from here."

He held her eyes, and she wasn't sure she could have looked away if she'd wanted. How could she be so drawn to this man who had arrested her brother and turned her world topsy-turvy?

"Miss Covington, I know you wish I'd leave you alone. Please understand, I'm just doing my job." His voice was husky, and its deep timbre tickled her ears. She felt betrayed by her own senses.

She wanted to sigh, but thank heavens she had the wherewithal to abstain from such a senseless show of femininity. Instead, she drew her shoulders back and lifted her chin. "Then why won't you consider the possibility that you have the wrong man? Isn't it your job to investigate all possibilities?" Her voice came out softer, thicker than she'd intended. What was it about this man?

Perhaps it was the laudanum. Yes, that must be it. But wait—no. She hadn't taken it yet. His eyes flickered, and she wasn't sure if it was compassion or something far more disturbing she saw there. For a moment she wondered if he'd kiss her.

The absurdity of the thought was just what she needed to bring her to her senses. She pulled her eyes away, mumbled curt thanks for his help and stumbled to her room. She needed to lie down. Needed to think.

She needed to pray.

Rett had just settled into one of the cozy chairs in the hotel lobby when he felt a tap on the shoulder. It was Ray.

"Where is she?" Ray asked.

"In her room. Probably asleep by now. Doc gave her some laudanum."

"Laudanum! Why?"

"She fell in the alley behind Main Street and scratched herself pretty bad with an old nail."

"What was she doing in the alley? Did she meet someone there?"

Rett chuckled. "More like she was trying to get away from someone."

"Did you see who?"

"Yeah. Big tall guy. Wore a hat, boots."

"That describes half the men in Houston," Ray said, concern etching his face.

"Oh, and he wore a Ranger's badge."

Ray's concern turned to confusion, and Rett grinned. "She was avoiding me. It seems I'm not her favorite person." The truth of the statement bothered Rett more than he wanted to admit.

The chair next to Rett creaked as Ray lowered himself into it. "So Doc gave her laudanum. She ought to sleep pretty hard tonight."

"That's what I'm thinking."

Ray propped his boots on the tapestry ottoman and laid his head back against the overstuffed plush chair. "Ahhhh. This feels good to my back."

"It still bothering you?"

"Yeah. That horse bucked me pretty hard. Doc says it'll likely always give me trouble." Ray shifted, then relaxed more. "I've gotta get me one of these chairs."

"What do you have going for the rest of the night?"

"I'll leave here in a few minutes, go back and guard the prisoner. Why?"

"You stay here. I'll take guard duty. Elizabeth will probably sleep all night, and you can rest your back. This is a lot more comfortable than those wooden chairs at the jail."

Ray's face protested, but the rest of his body sank deeper into the chair. "You don't have to do that."

"It's no problem. You can owe me one."

"If you're sure…okay."

Rett wasn't sure he wanted to leave Elizabeth to anyone else, but this was going to be an easy night. Might as well let Ray have a little relief. Rett stood, grabbed his hat from the side table and nodded to his friend. "Try not to get too comfortable."

"Too late."

A few minutes later, Rett was back at the jail. The Rangers had their own office outside of town, but with a prisoner like Hardy, they didn't want to leave it all to the sheriff's office. Fortunately, the Rangers had always had a good relationship with Houston's local law enforcement. That wasn't always the case with other agencies. The Texas Rangers were a unique, civilian force, and some lawmen felt the Rangers infringed on their territory.

Hardy was awake, lying on his bunk, staring at the ceiling. The dim light from the kerosene lamp made flickering shapes on the ceiling, but Rett wondered if Hardy even noticed. He seemed far away.

"Can I get you anything?" Rett asked him.

His voice seemed to startle Hardy, and the man sat up on his bunk. "No, thank you. Have you seen my sister? Is she all right?"

"Miss Covington is fine. She scraped herself on a nail, but she's seen a doctor, and it's all been taken care of."

"She was hurt? What happened? What was she doing?"

Rett didn't answer. He didn't want to give this man too much information.

Hardy stood, ran a hand through his disheveled hair, then walked to the bars and grabbed one with each hand. He leaned his forehead against one of them, and his face looked downright defeated.

Funny. Everything Rett had heard about Hardy had him as a rude, foul-talking belligerent when it came to law officers. Yes, he could behave like a gentleman, but not when he dealt with the law. More and more, things about this arrest weren't settling right with Rett.

Hardy released a long, slow breath, then looked at Rett. "Look, mister. I know you're just doing your job. I've told you I'm not Hardy, but you're not listening. So will you just promise me one thing?"

This should be interesting. "What's that?"

"Watch out for Elizabeth. I know she seems self-assured. She can come on like a bull when she's mad. But she's actually lived a very sheltered life. Make sure she gets home okay if anything happens to me."

"I'm not sure Miss Covington wants me looking after her."

"She hasn't got anybody but me. If…if I hang, she'll be alone in the world. Just promise me you'll look out for her, okay?"

Rett wasn't about to promise this man anything. But truth be known, the idea of looking after Miss Elizabeth Covington sounded very appealing indeed.

The sun streamed in Elizabeth's window, stirring her from a deep sleep. She'd taken only half the recommended dose of laudanum—she hadn't wanted to feel sluggish this morning. But judging from the placement of the sun in the sky, she'd slept later than she'd intended.

A glance at the clock by her bed told her she was correct. Ten to eight! She had to meet Amelia downstairs in ten minutes. She sat up a little too quickly and immediately regretted it. The room spun, or maybe it was her head spinning. Either way, it wasn't a pleasant feeling.

She lay back on the pillow to keep from falling back. Once the spinning stopped, she savored a deep, slow breath. This time she took it nice and easy, letting her feet fall over the side of the bed, then pushing herself up slowly. She sat there a minute, trying to decide the quickest way to ready herself.

The footboard provided the perfect place to push herself to a standing position. Still gripping the iron post, she moved to the dressing table and dropped to the stool. A clean rag lay beside the washbasin, and she dipped it into the water and ran it across her face and neck.

That felt nice.

At this rate, she'd never be downstairs in time to

meet Amelia. Pulling her boots on, she noticed the nail wound wasn't nearly as angry looking as it had been last night. It was still sore, though.

As quickly as possible, which wasn't very quickly at all, she pulled a clean dress over her head and buttoned it. Her brush got caught in a couple of tangles, and she finally pulled her hair into a chignon, tangles and all. They'd be hidden beneath her hat anyway. As soon as her meeting was over, she'd come back up here and do a better job.

Her hat ended up just a little crooked, but it would have to do. She finished her morning routine and looked at the clock: 8:05 a.m. Not bad. Hopefully, Amelia would still be there.

Navigating the stairs was harder than she'd expected. Well, she'd have to get over that. She had work to do. *God, guide my steps today. Show me what to do.* She'd meant to pray herself to sleep last night but hadn't anticipated the fast-working effects of the laudanum. She thought she remembered muttering a *Dear God*, and that was it. What was that about the Spirit interceding for us when we didn't know what to say? She hoped that was the case when one was too tired to pray.

Amelia was already seated in a corner, sipping tea. Her face lit up when she saw Elizabeth. "I ordered you some coffee. I hope you don't mind—I figured we could both use some extra verve today."

Coffee instead of tea? Well, when in Rome… "That will be fine. Thank you for thinking of me." Elizabeth seated herself and placed the linen napkin in her lap, then took a sip of the black liquid.

Mercy, that was strong stuff.

Amelia laughed out loud, and Elizabeth realized she must have scrunched her face at the bitter drink. "Here. Try some cream and sugar. I have to drink mine like a twelve-year-old. One of these days, I guess I really should try to grow up and drink it black, but I figure, why bother? It's so much better this way." Amelia proceeded to add cream to Elizabeth's coffee until it looked like more cream than coffee. Then she spooned four—make that five—heaping teaspoons of sugar into the mix.

Elizabeth took another sip. It tasted like dessert for breakfast! "Delicious," she told her new friend.

Amelia nodded, a hint of satisfaction in her smile. "Okay. Now that that's settled, let's get to work. I figured we could start by letting Mr. Thomas know about the exclusive. He'll probably bite his cigar in two when he learns I'm to do the interview. But he won't fire me. Then he wouldn't get his story."

Elizabeth wished she could feel some of the excitement Amelia felt. But what was a career-boosting opportunity for Amelia was quite possibly the worst thing that had ever happened to Elizabeth. And Evan, for that matter.

Amelia ceased her rattling when Elizabeth didn't respond. "Forgive me. I'm being insensitive. I know this is hard for you, but when you hear my news, I know you'll feel encouraged."

"News?"

"Yes! I stopped by the newspaper office this morning, about an hour ago. Mr. Thomas was already there, and he had copies of some official telegrams."

A portly waiter interrupted them. "What may I get you ladies?"

Elizabeth hadn't even looked at the menu, but she didn't have to. She ordered two eggs over easy and a piece of dry toast. Amelia placed her order, and the man left.

"Telegrams?" Elizabeth asked.

"Yes. It seems there were some murders yesterday near Hemphill, Texas. That's east of here."

East? Hadn't Mavis said Hardy had gone east?

Amelia leaned forward. "And you'll never guess who they think committed them."

Elizabeth's breath caught in her throat, and her pulse soared. "Hardy," she whispered, though she wasn't sure if any sound made it past her lips. "We have to find him."

Chapter 8

The door banged open and Rett jumped in his chair. He hadn't been asleep; his eyes were open. But after watching Hardy sleep all night, his mind had kind of zoned into a sleeplike stupor.

"Get out here. You've gotta see this," Cody said, and Hardy stirred on his bunk. Rett rolled his neck from side to side to work the kinks out, and his joints popped and cracked as he stood. Why didn't somebody spring for a more comfortable chair? Oh, yeah. Because you weren't supposed to get too comfortable while guarding a prisoner.

"What is it?" His voice was gravelly from not talking all night, and he could practically taste his foul breath. Four cups of coffee and no sleep would do that.

"Look at this."

Rett took the telegraph Cody shoved at him. "'Three

men killed Tuesday near the Louisiana border, in Hemphill—Hardy suspected.'" He examined the date. This morning. That meant the men were killed yesterday.

Oh, man.

"That means we really do have the wrong guy," Rett whispered.

"It means we *might* have the wrong guy. Or it could be a trick to get us to release him. Or some other killer is framing Hardy. It could mean a lot of things." Cody took the telegraph and studied it.

"You showed Ray?"

"I thought you were Ray. Where is he? I thought you were at the hotel all night, and he was here."

"We traded."

"You gave up beauty duty to watch Hardy sleep? You're dumber than I thought."

The outer door swung open, and in walked Sheriff Goodman. "Hangin's all set for Saturday, boys. The judge is on his way as we speak."

"Uh, we may need to postpone the hanging. Look at this." Cody held out the paper, and Sheriff Goodman took it.

"So?" the sheriff said.

"What do you mean, 'so?'" Rett asked. He didn't have a good feeling.

"Look, boys. I've been real tolerant of you all hanging around my office, feeling the need to guard my prisoner. Rett, I know you're the one who brought Hardy in. But the truth is he was arrested in my precinct. He's my prisoner. And word's out that he's here. If we don't act swiftly, we'll have a riot on our hands."

"Tom, we can't hang an innocent man just to satisfy

your constituents." Rett knew the sheriff didn't like to be called by his first name. Maybe that was why he did it. Probably not the wisest choice.

The sheriff's eyes hardened, his jaw tightened, and something about his nostrils reminded Rett of a charging bull. "That's Sheriff Goodman to you, and don't you forget it. Look, boys—" emphasis on the word *boys* told Rett just how annoyed the man was "—that's the real Hardy. You know it and I know it. This—" he waved the telegram in the air "—is just a ploy. Probably some of Hardy's gang creating a distraction so we'll release him. The hanging is scheduled for Saturday."

Rett and Cody looked at one another. Rett sure wished Ray were here. He had a way with the sheriff.

"Of course, if you were to prove me wrong and bring in the real Hardy before Saturday, that would be fine by me. As long as somebody by the name of Hardy hangs."

Cold slivers pulsed through Rett's chest, and he could feel sweat bead on his brow. This wasn't like Goodman. He had his quirks, but Rett had never known the man to be unreasonable. "You'd really hang an innocent man?"

"Of course I wouldn't. I would never do that. I plan to hang a ruthless killer. And it's going to happen this Saturday."

Amelia averted her eyes, and Elizabeth knew there was more. "I wanted to save that news for last. Me and my big mouth."

"For last? You mean there's more news?" Elizabeth

watched the other woman twist the napkin in her lap and knew the news must not be good. "What is it?"

"Well…" Amelia took a deep breath, then met Elizabeth's eyes. "They've scheduled the hanging for this Saturday."

"Without a trial?"

"No…apparently the judge is on his way. There will be a trial, and as soon as a guilty verdict is rendered, they'll proceed with the hanging."

"What?" Elizabeth's stomach roiled, and suddenly she wasn't hungry anymore. "Sounds like they've already made up their minds!"

Amelia nodded. "They have. Not just the sheriff, Elizabeth. The locals are in a frenzy. Many of them have known some of Hardy's victims. A local rancher is first cousin to one of them. People want justice, and they want it now."

"But…but surely now that there's evidence Hardy is in East Texas, they'll calm down."

"I don't think so, Elizabeth. It's just not the way things work here. There will be a riot if Hardy isn't hanged within the week. They all want to believe your brother is Hardy."

Elizabeth felt as if someone had reached into her chest with both hands, grabbed her heart and squeezed the lifeblood from her. "I have to go, right now." She stood, banging the table and causing her coffee to slosh on the white tablecloth. Her linen napkin fell to the floor.

"Wait! Now? Can't you eat something first?"

"I'll eat later. I have to see Mr. Herrington." Elizabeth waved to the waiter, and he came right over.

"Please cancel my order, and bill the coffee to my room—I'm in 217."

"Yes, ma'am," the man said.

Amelia took one last swig of coffee and rose. "I'm coming with you."

Elizabeth weaved her way through the restaurant as fast as her long legs would take her. She turned when she reached the lobby, and she realized Amelia was practically running to keep up. Oh, well. She'd have to run. This was important.

"Where are we going, again?" Amelia asked.

"To see Mr. Herrington. Evan's lawyer. Surely we can use this new information to release Evan or at least postpone the trial." She pushed open the lobby door and ran straight into Rett Smith.

"We've got to stop meeting like this," he said, but this time, Elizabeth didn't acknowledge the man who had caused so much angst. She just pushed past him onto the sidewalk and ran all the way to Stanley Herrington's office.

By the time she reached her destination, she was huffing and puffing. The door was locked. Where was he? It was nearing 9:00 a.m. Why wasn't he at work?

The reporter from yesterday—Cooper, Rett thought her name was—followed Elizabeth full speed out the door and down the street. He had a pretty good idea where they were headed.

Ray sauntered toward him, looking well rested. "What's going on?" Rett showed him the telegram. Ray let out a few mild expletives, but even the mild ones were unusual for Ray, who was in church every chance he got. "Well, what are you waiting for? Go!"

The two men followed the women, though Rett wasn't sure what they'd do when they caught them. Sure enough, Elizabeth and that Cooper woman stood outside Stanley Herrington's office. Elizabeth had her face cupped in her hands, pressed against the window.

Rett and Ray stopped a few doors down, then made their way across the street for a better view. No reason to let the ladies know they'd been followed. Not yet, anyway.

If Rett hadn't been so concerned about the outcome of this case, and so burdened with a growing guilt over possibly arresting the wrong man, he would have laughed out loud at the scene that played before him. As it was, he couldn't help but smile as Stanley approached his office, unlocked the door with only a cursory glance at Elizabeth and went inside.

Elizabeth didn't even notice the man until he was inside his office, and she jumped, which brought a little chuckle from Ray. Elizabeth wasted no time entering the building, followed by the reporter. A moment later, Rett watched Stanley open the door again, and the reporter exited. Good for him.

The small woman leaned against the window, and it didn't take her long to spot the two Rangers across the street. That was when she straightened herself to her full height, which wasn't much, and marched straight across the road to Rett and Ray. "Good day, Ranger Smith."

"Miss Cooper." Rett nodded. Why did he have a bad feeling about this?

Ray shifted, and Cooper held out a tiny hand. "Amelia Cooper, of the *Houston Daily*."

"Ray Davis, Texas Ranger. Pleased to meet you, ma'am."

"I suppose you two have figured out by now you have the wrong man," she said. The woman looked so innocent. So childlike. But once she opened her mouth, Rett felt as though he was dealing with a miniature barracuda.

"What makes you say that?" Ray asked. Good thing Ray was here. He always seemed to know how to handle these things.

"Now, Ranger Davis. Don't tell me you haven't heard the real Hardy was spotted in Hemphill, Texas, just yesterday. He even killed three men there. So when are you going to release Evan Covington?"

Ray's eyes crinkled around the corners in that way he had of making you think he was smiling when he really wasn't. "Look, Miss Cooper. I don't know what you've heard, but I can assure you we have everything well under control."

"You didn't answer my question," she persisted.

Just then the door to Stanley Herrington's office swung open, and Elizabeth and Stanley took off toward the sheriff's office.

"It's been nice talking to you, ma'am, but we've gotta run." Ray tipped his hat, and Rett did likewise before they took off trailing Elizabeth again. Why they bothered staying out of sight, he didn't know. Elizabeth knew her every move was watched, of that he was sure.

The sheriff's office might have been Grand Central Depot, as crowded as it was. Stanley Herrington demanded to see his client. Sheriff Goodman argued that he'd have to wait until visiting hours. Elizabeth paced back and forth, her fists in balls. Cody sat in the desk chair, leaning forward, watching the whole thing as if it were a circus.

Finally, Elizabeth marched right up to the sheriff and pointed her finger in his face. "Listen here, Sheriff Goodman. You can't keep my brother from a fair trial. I'll have every lawyer, as well as every newspaper from here to Boston, on your case. I know you have your posted visiting hours—" she gestured to the handwritten sign on the front wall "—but since you're apparently planning to hang an innocent man just four days from now, I'm sure you can find it in your heart to make an exception."

She stood there, glowering down at the sheriff as he trembled with anger. It didn't help that she was taller than Goodman; little did she know she'd probably never get her way if she humiliated him.

Ray tapped Rett on the elbow and gave him the look that meant he was about to do something, and he needed Rett to back him up. Rett nodded, and Ray stepped forward, wedging himself between Elizabeth and the sheriff.

"Excuse me, Sheriff, but there's a matter that needs attention outside the saloon. I could use your help," said Ray.

"I'm a little busy now, Davis. Can't you use one of your boys?"

"Well, I could, but I think this needs someone with a little more...experience. Do you mind?"

About that time, the door banged open again and Miss Cooper walked in. "What did I miss?"

Annoyance flashed across Sheriff Goodman's face. "Oh, all right. I need to get out of this zoo anyway.

Cody, Rett, I trust you all can handle things here for a short time?"

"Yes, sir!" both men chimed. The group watched Ray and the sheriff leave, watched them walk past the windows toward the saloon.

As soon as they were out of view, Rett said, "Mr. Herrington, Miss Covington, please come with me. We need to hurry."

The two followed Rett through the double doors to where Hardy was jailed, and Elizabeth pushed past the men to Hardy. Rett cleared his throat. "I'm sorry, ma'am, but you'll have to keep your distance."

Her eyes sent him a slow burn, but she obeyed. "Evan, they spotted Hardy in East Texas."

Hardy stood, a grin spreading across his face. "That's great news. So am I a free man?"

Herrington stepped forward. "Not yet. They'll have to prove it was actually Hardy who was spotted. And there's bad news, too."

"Bad news?" Hardy's brows lifted as he clutched the bars.

"Yes. Your hanging has been scheduled for Saturday."

"What? Without a trial? That's illegal!"

Herrington explained the process to Hardy, or Evan, or whoever he was. Rett wasn't so sure anymore. One thing he was sure of, though, was that justice moved more swiftly in Texas than in other parts of the country. If they were to make good and sure the right man was hanged, they'd have to move fast.

Elizabeth hated the look of disbelief on Evan's face. She knew her own face mirrored the same expression.

She'd heard Texas law was more vigilante than due process, and at one time that had seemed exciting to her. Not anymore.

She turned away so Evan wouldn't see how frightened she was and realized Rett was watching her. Had she really found him attractive? Right now all she saw was the dolt who'd arrested her brother by mistake.

Herrington talked to Evan in a low voice, and she tried to paste on a confident facade for Evan's sake. Rett approached, and she sucked in a sharp breath. She might have felt some type of chemistry with him— only briefly!—last night. But today it was more like the fizzled-out remains left behind in the beaker. A useless, foul-tasting memory.

"You know we'll investigate this report thoroughly, Miss Covington. As a matter of fact, I feel confident Ray's gonna send either me or Cody to East Texas before the morning's up."

"Forgive me, Ranger Smith," she hissed, "but I think you'll understand when I tell you I don't place much confidence in the Texas Rangers. What happens when you don't find the real Hardy?" Her voice was low, but she knew he couldn't mistake the challenge there.

"You mean if we don't find him. If Hardy's out there, we'll find him. I promise you that."

"You sound very sure of yourself, Ranger Smith. Just as sure as you sounded yesterday when I tried to tell you you had the wrong man." She didn't attempt to hide the steel in her voice. Before he could respond, she whirled and took her place next to Mr. Herrington. She was done with the likes of Rett Smith. Her focus had to stay on Evan and how she could help him.

"I can assure you, Mr. Covington, I'll make sure every stone is turned." Mr. Herrington spoke in a slow Texas drawl, but he spoke with confidence. "Right now our best course is to delay the trial and thus the hanging. Unfortunately, when I was at the general store this morning, you were the talk of the town. Men are already volunteering to help erect the gallows."

Maybe she'd misjudged the old fogey. And maybe he was right—having a lawyer who knew the ins and outs of Texas justice was the best thing for Evan. "Mr. Herrington," she said when the man paused in his speech, "I am at your beck and call. Just tell me what you need me to do, and I'll do it." Elizabeth no longer felt she needed to direct the case. She just wanted to help.

"You'd be wise to use her, Mr. Herrington." The pride in Evan's eyes was almost more than Elizabeth could handle, and she swallowed hard to try to diminish the lump in her throat. "If she were a man, she'd be a formidable lawyer. Even better than I am."

The door creaked and Cody stuck his head in. "Ray and the sheriff are headed this way. Y'all need to clear out."

Elizabeth rolled her eyes before she could stop herself. Nanny Carolyn would have had a fit. But the way things were done here in the Lone Star State wasn't right. If something didn't happen soon, Evan very well could be joining Papa before his time.

Mr. Herrington waddled to one of the chairs lining the front wall and sat—more like plopped himself into it—leaving one chair between himself and Amelia. He patted the empty seat, and Elizabeth joined them, feeling a bit crowded next to the lawyer's wide girth.

In no time Ray and Sheriff Goodman entered. "I don't see why you had to drag me down there, Ray. There was clearly nothing of importance going on."

The sheriff seemed to notice them for the first time and offered a smug sneer. "Almost ten o'clock, Stanley. I'm glad you waited, though it seems you'd have been better off waiting down the street in your office. But to each his own."

Ray leaned on the counter and motioned for Cody and Rett to join him. He spoke in a murmur, but Elizabeth trained her ears on the conversation.

"One of you needs to follow this lead. If it pans out, we'll have to bring the real Hardy back here. Otherwise, whoever that is in there is in big trouble," Ray said. "I'd send you both, but I've been summoned to a trial in Austin. I need to head out tomorrow. One of you needs to hold things down here."

"I'll go," Cody and Rett said in unison, and Rett shook his head at Cody with force. "I need to go, Cody. I'm the one who started this mess. If it is the wrong guy, I need to straighten it out myself."

At that point Elizabeth knew what she needed to do more than she'd ever known anything in her life. She stood to her feet and blurted, "I'm coming, too!"

Chapter 9

She had to be joking. Rett had figured out Elizabeth wasn't an ordinary woman. But surely she knew going after Hardy was out of the question for her. Even Herrington blustered at the idea. The lawyer hefted himself to his feet and urged Elizabeth to stay out of the conversation.

Not that she listened. "I can ride. I'm actually quite adept. I've been trained in equestrianism since I was five."

Herrington tugged at her sleeve, whispered something in her ear, but she pulled away. That was when Ray spoke up. "I know this is important to you, ma'am, but we can't allow a civilian to get involved in a mission like this. Male or female."

At that moment, her shoulders looked to be made of nails, her jaw of iron, and her eyes held a force that Rett didn't want to cross. She reminded him of the time he'd stumbled upon a litter of cougar kittens, only to hear their mother screaming from a limb above him. Good thing he'd had his rifle loaded, or he might not be standing here today.

Herrington whispered something else, and she returned to her chair, though nothing about her demeanor changed. All the while that Cooper woman looked to be enjoying the show.

Ray nodded to the sheriff. "It looks like you can handle things here. One of us will stop by in a little while." Then he motioned for Cody and Rett to follow him. They hadn't spent much time at their own office in the past couple of days. At least there they'd have some control over who heard their conversation.

The three men walked the six blocks in silence, but Rett's thoughts were far from silent. It would feel good to get out of town for a few days. He'd neglected Bear; his horse had been stabled at the livery since early the morning before. And this was one mission he couldn't afford to fail. If he'd truly arrested the wrong man, it was his place to put things right.

And he couldn't completely rein in his wandering thoughts that maybe, just maybe if he was wrong, if Elizabeth was telling the truth…maybe if he found the real Hardy, then perhaps he could pursue something with Elizabeth.

No. That was the dumbest thought he'd had in a while. She'd never consider him now, even if he helped free her brother. Not when he'd been the one to cause all this confusion in the first place.

Ray unlocked the office door and let the other two enter first, then locked the door behind him. No use taking any chances on someone barging in. "How long do you need to get ready?"

Rett ran through his mental checklist. "I'll need to stop by the general store for a few supplies, and by my room for some fresh clothes. Millie at the boarding-house always has some extra biscuits on hand. I'd say I can be ready in an hour, maybe an hour and a half."

Ray pulled the telegrams from his pocket—he'd taken them from Goodman's desk, and the man would be none too happy about it. "According to this one, Hardy shot three men at a saloon just south of Hemp-hill. It's a two-day ride—no time to waste. Cody, check the post office and see if anything new has come in."

"Yes, sir." Cody was out the door in no time.

Ray's eyes held a distant look, as if he wanted to say something important but didn't know how. "You know I'd go myself if I could."

"I know. But even if you went, I'd go with you."

"You have any idea how many lawmen Hardy's killed?"

"A lot."

Ray toyed with one of the telegrams, rolling it into a scroll, then unrolling it and rolling it back again. After a minute he dropped the paper onto his desk, leaned back and looked at Rett. "Be careful, okay? We can't afford to lose you."

"I will."

Stanley Herrington took Elizabeth's elbow and practically dragged her back to his office. "What were you thinking? They're never going to agree to you going with them. You're foolish to suggest such a thing."

"I... But—"

"No buts. If you want us to win this case, you're going to have to learn to keep your mouth shut. Listen to everything, but say as little as possible."

Now, who did that remind her of? She'd have never dreamed her father had much in common with the likes of Stanley Herrington, but the man was sounding a whole lot like Papa.

He looked at Amelia, who had tagged along behind them. "You. Do you want to help or not?"

"Yes, sir! Of course I want to help."

"Can we trust you?"

"Of course."

Herrington eyed her up and down, as if taking her measure. "I know you're a reporter, or want to be one, anyway. I'd better not hear of any funny business, you hear? You help us get what we want, and we'll help you get what you want. But you have to play by my rules, got it?"

"Yes, sir!"

"All right, then. You go on down to the Rangers' office, see what they're up to. Follow Smith—you know which one he is?"

Amelia nodded.

"Okay. Don't let him out of your sight. Report back to me as soon as you know something that seems worth knowing."

"Aye, aye, Captain!" Amelia saluted, and under any other circumstances, Elizabeth would have laughed. As soon as the door closed behind Amelia, Elizabeth opened her mouth to argue.

"Not a word, missy. If you're going to Hemphill, we don't have time for your blustering and blowing."

His eyes held a sparkle, mixed with tinge of… Was that worry?

"What? I thought you said—"

"I never said you shouldn't go, though you shouldn't. It's a foolish, absurd plan if I ever heard one, and dangerous, too. But I know if I don't help you, you'll probably head out on your own anyway. I know your kind. So if you're going to follow Smith out there, we need you to be as safe—and as prepared—as possible." He sat in his chair, leaned over with some effort and opened his bottom desk drawer.

When Elizabeth saw what he held in his palm, her breath left her as if she'd been punched in the stomach. In his hand was a tiny handgun. It might as well have been a stick of dynamite, for all she cared.

"This is a Deringer. You know how to shoot one of these things?"

"Yes," she lied. "Well…no. But how hard can it be?"

He grunted and sent her a look she didn't really want to interpret. "Point and pull the trigger. Be careful what you point at, though. It'll shoot your foot just as easily as it'll shoot Hardy." He offered it to her, and she pinched it between her thumb and index finger and held it at arm's length, as if it might bite her.

"Is it loaded?" she asked.

"It will be. Here, let me show you how."

She handed the gun back to him, only too glad to be rid of it. Could she really use such a weapon against another human being? *Oh, God*, she prayed. *Please don't let me have to use it.*

The lecture lasted nearly twenty minutes, with him showing her how to load, how to fire, how to set it at an empty chamber to keep it from firing by accident.

The lesson ended when Amelia burst in the door. She gasped when she saw the gun and looked from the weapon to Elizabeth, then back at the weapon. Then, as if remembering her assignment, she said, "He's leaving within the hour."

"What?" Elizabeth and Herrington exclaimed.

"I followed Ranger Smith to the mercantile and then to his boardinghouse. He's getting supplies. But while I was waiting outside the mercantile, I saw the other one—what's his name? Cody something, Wilson, I think—talking to him. So I walked down the block, where I could hear both of them, and sure enough, Ranger Wilson told him he needed to leave before 10:00 a.m."

"Run to the livery and rent Miss Covington the hardiest horse they have," Herrington told Amelia.

"I've already done it," Amelia said, a cloak of smugness around her. "Her name's Sugar, and she'll be ready any minute."

"Good work. That doesn't give us much time, though." Herrington pulled several bullets from a box and dropped them into a black velvet drawstring bag. Then he dropped the pistol on top of them and pulled the string tight. "Keep this with you at all times, and don't hesitate to use it."

Elizabeth took the gun with shaking hands and dropped it into her reticule. For all her bravado, she was starting to realize she was in over her head—and it seemed she was sinking deeper with each passing moment.

Rett didn't have much time. Fortunately, he didn't need much. That was the life of a Ranger—knowing how to leave at a moment's notice, with everything you needed to survive. The iron weight he felt at the thought he'd arrested the wrong man—and now he was about to hang—just wouldn't go away. He'd never been much of a praying man, though he did believe in God. He'd even walked the aisle of the First Baptist Church when he was a teenager, and he'd meant it. He really didn't know what had happened, but somehow he'd just drifted away.

Well, he supposed now was as good a time as any to reintroduce himself to the good Lord. He prayed, even as he packed. He supposed God would understand that in this case, Rett just didn't have time to get down on his knees.

God, I know it's been a while, and I'm real sorry about that. Now, where did I put my brown socks? There they are. Anyway, God, I do want to thank You for being so good to me. You've brought me through a lot and protected me when I didn't deserve your protection. How many bullets?

He loaded the entire box of bullets into his pack, plus another half-empty box. Better safe than sorry. *God, I'm not sure what to think. I don't know if that fellow back in the jail is Hardy or not, but You know, don't You? God, if he's not Hardy, if I've truly arrested an innocent man, please help me to set things right. Don't let an innocent man die for my mistake.*

He heard hammering outside. He walked over to the open window and leaned out, trying to see what all the commotion was about. There, in the center of town, about a dozen men sawed and banged. They'd drawn quite a crowd, too. Probably another three or four dozen people stood around, gossiping and pointing. Above the gallows, some kind of long banner was being hung. What did it say?

A man stretched out the other end of the banner and nailed it to the opposite side. Of course, it would be taken down before the hanging, but it just proved how anxious the people of Houston were to be rid of a ruthless killer.

The sign read Die James Weston Hardy.

The tightness in his stomach became more pronounced, and Rett realized he hadn't eaten since last night. Good thing. If he had, it would have turned to stone by now.

God, You know better than I do that things are really messed up down here. I'll do my part, but I'm not sure it'll be enough. So any help You can offer along the way, I'd sure appreciate it.

He thought about asking God to give him a chance with Elizabeth, too, but he figured that could wait. First things first.

Elizabeth stood paralyzed in the center of town and thought she might lose her breakfast. Good thing she hadn't eaten any. It was pell-mell: men hammering with a vengeance, people jeering and cheering at the sign with Hardy's name. Imagine cheering over someone's death!

And that someone was Evan, only they didn't know it. She just stood there, one hand at her throat, the other covering her mouth to hold back the scream. She knew having a breakdown right here and now would only aggravate the crowd and turn it into an outright mob.

Amelia put her arm around Elizabeth's waist and tugged her gently at first, then with more force. "Come on. We've got to get you ready to go. There's not much time."

Elizabeth allowed herself to be led away toward her hotel. Mr. Herrington had laid out a plan for her. She was to wear her plainest dress until she was beyond the trail of towns from here to Huntsville, in order to blend in. After some discussion, they'd decided she would leave before Rett if possible. She could wait for him in the next town, then follow behind. By that time, he'd have stopped looking for her.

Herrington had suggested she purchase some clothing suitable for the trail once they got to the more difficult part of the journey. Fortunately, she had some. She'd packed her dungarees when Evan told her they were going to Texas. It had just seemed right somehow.

Little had she known.

In her room she and Amelia made quick work of her packing. "Give me some money," Amelia said. "I'll stop by the mercantile and get a few things I think you might need. It will look suspicious if you go."

Elizabeth counted out more than enough cash and looked at the clock by her bed. How would she ever make it out of here before Rett? As soon as Amelia was gone, Elizabeth muttered a low, "Please, God. Please." She said it over and over, for no other words would come. "Please…"

In no time at all, Amelia returned, and Elizabeth looked at the clock again. Had fifteen minutes really passed? She must look a mess. A quick swipe of her comb, a few more hairpins and a hat, and she was as good as she was going to be.

"Better get moving." Amelia handed her a map with a route traced in red pencil. How had she done that so quickly? "The first part of the journey will be easy. Just follow the main path. When you get to Huntsville, find Sue's Restaurant. It's right on Main Street, and Rett will pass directly in front of it. Chances are, he'll stop there for a quick meal."

Elizabeth took the map, grabbed her pack and said, "Let's go."

Sugar was a gentle-looking mare, and Elizabeth liked her immediately.

"Oh, I almost forgot." Amelia pulled out a small brown bag and held it open. Sugar cubes. "You'll need these."

The horse took two from Elizabeth's hand and whinnied. Elizabeth was just about to mount when she spotted all three Rangers, deep in conversation. A weathered knapsack dangled from Rett's left hand, and with his right he held the lead to a stunning paint horse. She'd never make it out ahead of him. *Oh, God, I've never done anything like this before. Please help me. I'm afraid.*

A verse from her childhood passed through her mind, as if God Himself were reminding her: *"What time I am afraid, I will trust in thee," Psalm 56:3.* She said those words over and over in her mind, even as Amelia pulled her away from the depot and toward the sheriff's office.

"Guess you're not going to leave before him. You'll have to trail behind, catch up later. Why don't we stop by and set up that interview? If the sheriff sees you there, he'll have less reason to be suspicious that you're following Ranger Smith." Amelia reached for her carpetbag and secured it to Sugar's pack, then led the horse toward the jail while Elizabeth followed, trying to steady her gelatin knees. Sheriff Goodman didn't look pleased to see them. "Back so soon?" he asked.

"It's still visiting hours, sir, and we'd like to see Mr. Hardy, please."

"Whoa there. This isn't a hospital. It's not like you can just waltz in and see the patient anytime. His lawyer can visit anytime during those hours. Not you."

"I am doing a story on Mr. Hardy, and I must see him to interview him." Amelia didn't seem the least bit intimidated by the sheriff. Elizabeth, on the other hand, was as jumpy as a…a jumpy thing. See? She couldn't even think straight.

Sheriff Goodman laughed out loud, as if he was mocking Amelia. "You? Doing a story on Hardy? Well, come on back. This, I've gotta see." He held open the door for the ladies and followed them to Evan's cell.

"Hey, Hardy! You've got a couple of visitors. Miss Cooper here wants to do a story on you. Isn't that nice?" The man laughed and took a seat at the desk.

Evan stood and looked from Elizabeth to Amelia, then held his hand through the bar to shake hands. "I'm Evan Covington."

"Hands inside the cell at all times, Hardy," the sheriff told him, and Evan withdrew his hand.

"Evan, this is Amelia Cooper. She's been a great help to me, and she works for the *Houston Daily*."

Dawning understanding lit Evan's eyes. Newspapers held power. But Evan's eyes held something else as he rested his gaze on Amelia's perfect features. Not that Elizabeth was surprised. Even from the inside of a jail cell, it would be hard for any red-blooded male not to notice Amelia.

Elizabeth shifted from one foot to the other while Evan and Amelia made small talk. Why, it sounded more like a courting session than an interview. She did not have time for this. Five or so minutes passed, and Elizabeth tapped Amelia and lifted her eyebrows in a way she hoped her friend would catch. She needed to go.

Amelia nodded, then said, "Sheriff, I just remembered an important appointment. Would you mind letting me continue this interview in about an hour?"

"Visiting hours will be over by then."

"All right. Tomorrow morning, then?"

Sheriff Goodman laughed, a deep laugh that held more disdain than cheer. "Miss Cooper, you come on back first thing in the morning, I'll get you your interview. This should be good."

They exited the building and surveyed the thoroughfare. No Ranger in sight. Elizabeth inhaled deeply and mounted Sugar as if she'd ridden the horse many times before. Despite her riding ability, she knew this was more than a long shot. It was her only shot.

Chapter 10

"You fellows know what's become of Miss Covington?"

"Last I saw, she and that reporter lady were running toward the jail," Ray answered. "I wouldn't worry too much about her at this point. Let her follow you if she wants. She won't make it far."

Rett had his doubts. Regardless, he didn't have time to bother with the likes of Elizabeth Covington. Not if he was going to track down the real Hardy...or prove he was already in custody. He nodded at his partners, spurred Bear into a trot, then a run, and left Houston in his dust. The quicker he got out of sight, the less likely he'd have an unwanted follower.

For the next several hours, Rett polished his rusty conversation skills and conversed with the Almighty. He prayed for wisdom. He prayed for protection. Most of all, he prayed the truth would come out, and he could prove one way or another if the man he'd placed in jail was indeed an innocent man. *I don't think I could live with myself, Lord, if the wrong man goes to the gallows because of my mistake.*

Too many times during that long uninterrupted prayer, his mind wandered to a tall, stunning woman, and somewhere below the surface, his heart cried out for her, as well. After several hours on the trail, he approached Huntsville, and his mouth watered just thinking of Miss Sue's buttery rolls and her sweet tea that tasted more like dessert than anything else. Bear needed a break anyway.

He guided his steed to the watering trough in front of the restaurant and looped the reins around a post. No use trying to dust himself off; any attempt would only make it worse. He did dip his hands into the trough and rubbed them on his face. At least he tried.

"Well, mercy. If it ain't Ranger Rett!" Sue's voice floated through the restaurant's open window.

Rett turned, removed his hat, thought better of it considering how sweaty he was and replaced it. "Howdy, Miss Sue."

"What brings you into this little neck of the woods? I thought you were a big-city Ranger now. Did you miss us that much?"

Rett draped an arm around the short pudgy woman's shoulder. She was old enough to be his mother but seemed more like a sister. "I'm here on business, and I'm afraid I can't stay long. Just need a quick bite to eat and some water for Bear."

"Well, you just sit yourself down, and I'll fix you right up."

Rett tried to protest. He wanted only a little something to tie into a handkerchief and eat on the road. He didn't have time for a lengthy four-course meal. But Sue wasn't one to be deterred easily. Besides, he was tired, and he didn't need to ride himself into a heatstroke the first day on the trail.

Elizabeth loved this horse. What a doll! Sugar seemed to sense her desires before she even pulled the reins. How did this beauty end up in a livery stable as a rent horse? *Thank You, God. Amelia could have gotten me an old nag.*

As soon as she was out of sight of the Houston hubbub, Elizabeth tore off her hat and let her tangled mass of hair stream behind her, the wind to her face. It felt so good to be free. Had she ever felt this free in her life?

And then she felt guilty. How could she enjoy such freedom when Evan was imprisoned, awaiting his death? Gently, then a little less gently, she dug her heels into Sugar's flanks and leaned forward, urging the horse to move faster and faster. According to the map, Huntsville was still a hard ride ahead. Rett had left about a half hour before she had, and he had surely pressed his horse to the limit. There was no rest for the weary...at least not yet.

A couple hours and many prayers later, Elizabeth and Sugar rode into what must be Huntsville. In the center of town, just as Amelia had told her—or had it been Mr. Herrington?—was Sue's Restaurant. And tied to a post in front of the restaurant was Rett's paint horse.

She looped Sugar's reins around a post near the

water trough and stood for a moment admiring the Ranger's beautiful brown-and-white paint horse. Then she looked around for some other place to clean up and get a bite to eat. Revealing her presence to Rett at this point would only make him try harder to lose her. No. Best to remain hidden and follow in the shadows. She didn't know if she could pull it off, or for how long, but she had to try. Once they were well on their way, perhaps then she could make her presence known. Maybe.

Oh, mercy. Why didn't she have a better plan?

Because there was no time to think of one, that was why. This was her one chance to save her brother. No one else in this world had as much at stake in losing Evan as she did. She had to go. She had to find Hardy, or at least make sure Ranger Smith did. If she couldn't track the criminal herself, she could at least make sure Smith did his job.

A tall shadow fell across the restaurant doorway, and Elizabeth ducked into a barbershop.

"Can I help you, miss?"

Oh, dear. "Um...no, thank you. I was just...waiting for someone." She turned to see an aging bald man looking at her as if she were an escapee from the asylum. And considering the events of the past two days, she felt that assumption wasn't entirely unfounded. The man held a comb and a pair of scissors, and she remembered her hair. She used her fingers to gather the wayward tresses into a knot and wished she hadn't removed her hat. It was stuffed into the side of her saddlebag along with a canteen of water and some beef jerky. Thank goodness for Amelia.

* * *

Rett shouldn't have eaten that last bit of peach cobbler. He'd forced the smorgasbord of samplings down as quickly as possible so as not to hurt Sue's feelings, and now he could tell his stomach would pay for the crime. The woman placed a tall slice of carrot cake in front of him, but he pushed it back. "No more. I'm working. But it was delicious, as always."

"Well, here. Take this with you. It ain't much, but it'll keep you from starvin' out there. For a little while, anyway." She placed a cloth on the table with fried chicken, rolls and some oatmeal cookies and proceeded to tie it into a bundle.

"Much obliged. How much do I owe you?"

"It's on the house. You owe me another visit, just as soon as you can."

"Thanks, Sue." Rett tipped his hat to the woman, then gave her a one-armed hug before exiting. Bear seemed happy to be standing next to a beautiful mare… Was that Sugar?

He fought to hold the grin back. So she'd rented Sugar from the livery. This was perfect.

He'd hated to give Sugar up; she'd been such a loyal friend. But with the schedule he kept, he and Bear had left her alone too many hours, too many days. He'd known Ed at the livery would take good care of her. He'd even promised to rent her only to sweet-looking women who'd ride her gently and feed her lots of treats.

A quick scan of the area told him she must be hiding. Probably watching. Well, she could watch him ride away with her horse.

* * *

She turned her attention back to the sidewalk in front of Sue's. There he was, saying goodbye to some woman. Mounting his horse. Taking Sugar's reins in one hand... Wait! What was he doing?

There he went, in a cloud of dust, Sugar galloping beside. She burst out of the barbershop yelling, "Stop! Thief!"

The woman from the restaurant looked at her as if she were some kind of lunatic, and the barber, who had followed her outside, seemed to agree.

"That man just stole my horse!"

"Who, Rett? He's not a thief. He's a lawman. An honest one, too."

"She's right, Sue. It was her horse. I saw her ride into town on it." The barber surprised her by coming to her defense.

"Come to think of it, he just had the one horse when he showed up. But why would he steal her horse?" Sue spoke to the man with scissors as if Elizabeth weren't standing right there.

"Beats me."

"Mebbe he needed it."

"Still, don't seem right to take a woman's horse."

"No, it don't. I like Rett, but he oughtta know better." Sue looked at Elizabeth as if startled by her presence.

Elizabeth fingered the coin purse in her pocket. It carried some bills as well as coins. "Where can I get another horse?"

Both people pointed down the street to a sign that read Livery.

With a quick nod of thanks, Elizabeth took off as if

her boots had sprouted wings. The saloon-style doors hit the wall as she pushed through, out of breath, and said, "I need the fastest horse you've got. It's an emergency."

The man turned from what he was doing, looked at her, then at the wad of bills in her hand. Without a word, he walked to one of the stalls and led out an exquisite Appaloosa. That was sure to cost a pretty penny. Good thing she had lots of pennies.

"Name's Lucy. She's temperamental, but she's fast. Just don't spook her and she'll be fine. You sure you can handle her?"

"No. But I need her."

The man shrugged his shoulders, named his price and took her money. Within minutes she was on Rett's trail. And the combination of Elizabeth's temper and Lucy's speed did not bode well for one Ranger-turned-horse-thief.

Rett was still laughing at his own wit, sharp thinking and clever idea of stealing her horse. It had been so easy! And it wasn't as if he were really stealing it. He was protecting Elizabeth. It was for her own good. She should have known better than to come after him on some cockamamy renegade hunt. Not that the situation was cockamamie. But it would turn that way real quick with some helpless, scatterbrained woman tagging along.

Only Elizabeth wasn't any of those things. She seemed sincere in her belief that they had the wrong man. She was intelligent and determined, both qualities he admired in a woman. He felt kind of bad leaving her stranded in Huntsville, but he couldn't very well let her follow him into danger's path.

If there had been any hope she'd ever be attracted to him, it was gone now. By protecting her, he'd also alienated her. But the way he saw it, he didn't have a choice.

The afternoon sun blazed down, and he considered slowing the pace. He needed to cover as much territory as possible. And now he had Sugar to deal with. Next town, he'd drop her at the livery with instructions to return her to Houston.

Sugar whinnied, and Bear's ears flickered. Sounds of an approaching rider brought Rett's hand to his gun. Whoever it was was certainly in a hurry. Seconds later, a copse of brunette hair flew past him, then slowed.

Elizabeth.

"Ranger Smith. I believe you have something that belongs to me."

"Why can't you just stay put? I'm trying to get to the bottom of this. You're only going to slow me down. If that man back there really is your brother, you'd do best to let me handle this alone."

"I don't see it that way at all. I'm the one with the most to lose. I should be the one to find Hardy."

"Miss Covington. James Weston Hardy is a mean, cruel-hearted killer. If he gets hold of you, he won't kill you right away. He'll have his way with you first."

Elizabeth's face heated, but she refused to look away. Why, the gall of that man! Of all the rude, insensitive, common things to say. Well, if he thought he could embarrass her or scare her back to Houston, he had another think coming.

She thought of the Deringer tucked into the side of her boot. "I guess it's a good thing I know how to defend myself. Now give me my horse."

Rett gripped Sugar's reins and looked at Lucy. "Looks like you have a horse. Can't ride two at once."

That was a problem. Sugar was by far the better match for her riding skills. Still, Lucy was fast—the fastest horse she'd ever ridden. "Suit yourself, Ranger Smith. Give me my horse, or don't. Either way, I'm coming with you."

The Ranger looked from her to Lucy, then to Sugar. Then he removed his hat, wiped the sweat from his brow and heaved a great sigh. She could almost see a visible cloud of annoyance. After a brief pause that seemed to last forever, he replaced his hat. "Daylight's not gonna wait for us. We better get moving." With that, he clicked and nudged his horse. Sugar followed obediently, and Elizabeth tried not to read the horse's compliance as an act of betrayal.

So be it. Without further ado, she dug her heels into Lucy's flanks and followed the haze of dust ahead of her.

Good gravy, God. What am I gonna do now, with a woman and two extra horses? She's determined to come along. If I ditch her, she'll just find a way to follow me. And technically, she hasn't done anything illegal. I can't arrest her. Can I?

Rett played with that thought a moment, considered dropping her at some small-town jail along the way. At least in jail she'd be safe. But no, he couldn't watch her there, and he knew the fair treatment of prisoners wasn't a high priority with some lawmen. He couldn't take chances.

Best to keep her close so he could know what she was up to. So he could protect her if need be. *Why can't she get it through that thick head of hers, Lord, that she's only hindering my progress? She's hurting Evan's chances, not helping them.*

Evan. It was the first time he'd allowed himself to think of the prisoner as Evan. My, how she'd spun her charms on him. Even he was believing her story now. *God, help me. Show me the truth, and let Your justice win.*

They'd been riding nearly four hours. He looked over his shoulder. The Appaloosa was keeping up just fine, but Elizabeth looked worn. When she saw him looking at her, she sat up a little straighter in the saddle and lifted her chin.

"Need a break?" he called.

"No. Not unless you do."

Stubborn woman. He should have known. At least this was pine-tree country. No problem finding a shady place to rest. He guided the horses to a cozy grove to the left of the beaten trail and climbed down. A playful creek trickled through the pines, and lush clumps of grass offered refreshment for the horses.

Elizabeth followed suit. He noted the stiff way she walked. Her limp from yesterday's injury was still pronounced, and now she rubbed her lower back and hunched over, as if she couldn't stand straight. He pretended not to notice.

"Hungry?" he asked, spreading out Sue's cloth on a stump.

"No, thank you. I have my own." She walked over to Sugar and untied her fancy carpetbag. Who brought a carpetbag on the trail? She pulled out a pitiful little package of some cold, hard biscuits and beef jerky. Certainly not enough to last more than a day or two.

"Are you sure?" he asked. "I've got plenty." He gestured to the feast before him and noted a flash of longing in her eyes as she observed his spread.

But she only said, "No, thank you."

He tried not to watch as she unscrewed her canteen lid and nearly drained its contents. Tried not to watch as she drizzled a little of the clear liquid on her fingertips and rubbed it on her face and neck. Tried not to watch as she removed a hairbrush from her pack, turned her back to him and went to work smoothing her messy mane.

God help me. He finally turned his body in the opposite direction and finished his meal. He waited a few more minutes, giving her as much of a break as he dared, considering he had a villain to chase. At last he retied his cloth and stood to his feet. "Time to go."

To her credit, she didn't complain. Just stretched her arms, rubbed her back a bit and climbed into the saddle like an old pro. He couldn't help but notice as she mounted the horse that she wore denim pants under her skirts. *She must be sweltering.* "You're going to have to shed the skirts or the pants. You'll pass out if you don't."

"Why don't you let me worry about me, Ranger Smith? Concern yourself with finding Hardy and freeing my brother." She tossed her head, her hair now in a long braid down her back, a look of defiance in her eyes that said she'd never do a thing as long as he was the one who suggested it. Then she calmly drew up Lucy's reins as if she'd been waiting on him rather than the other way around.

He'd never met a more exasperating woman in his life.

Chapter 11

Every sound in the forest seemed amplified in Elizabeth's ears. A cricket chirped, and she worried it was a bear. Were there bears in this part of the country? The wind rustled the carpet of pine needles on the ground, and she thought it was a snake. Funny, when she'd camped with Papa and Evan, she'd never been this jumpy. But then, she'd had two men to protect her.

Of course, she knew Rett would protect her. But she wouldn't—couldn't—give him that satisfaction. No, she couldn't go crying to Rett like some ninny. She'd made her choice, and now she'd follow through like a big girl.

But since she refused to let Ranger Smith protect her, she decided there was no harm in keeping her other means of protection loaded and ready. Just in case.

The lawman sat with his back turned. At least he

had the manners to give her some privacy. They'd stopped half an hour before, and Rett had announced they'd camp here. Within ten minutes of stopping, the sun disappeared from view and left them in the twilight.

A shuffling behind her told her Rett was on the move. "I'll be back," he said. "Stay put. I'm going to look around." She watched as a tiny flame flickered, then grew as he lit another candle. Her eyes followed as he walked farther into the thick pines until the flame disappeared from view.

Now those sounds, those beautiful, horrible sounds of nature, taunted her from the shadows. She sat crosslegged in front of her own candle and pulled out the velvet pouch. Good thing she'd had Mr. Herrington and Amelia to prepare her for this trip. She'd been so addle brained this morning she would have forgotten nearly everything. With fear-inspired reverence, she shook three of the bullets into her hand. Better not drop any; she'd never find them again in the dark. She put two of them back into the velvet drawstring case and pulled out the pistol.

Her forehead tightened as she studied the gun. She felt her brows cinch together with concentration. Her lips pursed while she opened the barrel and snapped the bullet into place. *God, please don't let me have to use this. And if I do, let me hit the mark.* She leaned against the trunk of a tall evergreen, cradling the gun, and closed her eyes. Then opened them again, for fear something or someone would sneak up on her. Why did Rett have to leave her alone? And why did she care?

All those years she wanted to be free and rugged

and wild. *Never mind, God. I didn't mean it. I just want to go home to my nice soft bed, my nice locked doors, my nice safe life. With Evan.*

Evan. She must get hold of herself, for Evan.

A twig crackled. What was that? A bear? The back of her shoulders and neck tensed; the muscles in her legs felt as though they might snap. Was something there? Some living creature moved behind her, from the opposite direction Rett had gone. Had he circled around without her knowing it? Was it Hardy?

She aimed toward the sound and cocked the hammer. Pointing into the dark, she struggled to keep her voice steady and said, "Who's there?"

Could she shoot another person? Oh, dear Lord. She heard a voice, but the pounding in her heart prevented her from comprehending the words. He was coming toward her! *Oh, God, oh, God, oh, God*, she cried in her mind, fear keeping her from adding further thoughts to that prayer as her breath—and her heart—caught in her throat. She scrambled away from the towering figure, stumbling over her pack, dropping the pistol. It fired, and she heard a thud. Had it hit a tree? She hoped so. Please, not a person. She crawled, clawing at the ground as she tried to escape.

"Elizabeth!" the man said again, more forcefully this time. Wait! How did he know her name? She felt his hand on her shoulder, and she rolled over, kicking and hitting. She turned her face toward his arm and bit it—and the man yelped and pulled his arm away.

"Elizabeth! It's me, Rett!"

She took the opportunity to scramble farther away, then stood to her feet while her mind processed what she'd heard. Wait—Rett? "I…I can't see you," she finally managed to squeak.

The figure backed up, then lowered himself to pick up the candle she'd left on the stump. It really was Rett.

"You…you frightened me," Elizabeth said, though her voice came out shakier than she intended.

"You don't say. You nearly killed me!"

Elizabeth remembered her prayer that if she used the gun, she'd hit the mark. *Thank you, God, for not granting that request.* "I'm sorry. Are you all right?"

"Am I all right? What do you mean, am I all right? What in the world are you doing, pointing a gun at me?" The fire in Rett's eyes was intensified by the flickering candle. Perhaps a bear would have been more pleasant…

Her chin tilted upward, and she felt her jaw tighten. So what if she'd nearly shot him? He looked to be fine. How dare he speak to her that way, as if she had no right to defend herself? "Perhaps if you didn't sneak up on people, you wouldn't find yourself at the wrong end of a barrel."

He let loose a string of mild expletives under his breath. Not foul enough to embarrass her too much. She'd heard Papa and Evan use some of the same words when they thought she wasn't listening. Just strong enough to let her know how annoyed he was at her presence. Then he ran his fingers through his thick hair, and taut muscles pulled at his shirt. "This is no place for a—"

"A what? A woman? Let me tell you something, mister. A woman would have never arrested someone based on a fuzzy drawing. Now an innocent man is about to hang, so forgive me if I don't fully trust your ability to find the right man and clear this whole mess up." She knew her words stung, and she didn't care. He'd had no right to sneak up on her that way. No right to do a lot of the things he'd done in the past couple of days.

Rett dropped his arm. "I was going to say 'no place for a civilian,' but since you brought it up, yes. I agree. This is no place for a woman."

She wanted to throw something at him or hit him. But no. Violence would do no good. Especially since he was bigger. She released an angry breath and bit back more angry words. "Well, I'm here. And there's nothing you can do about it. I'm going to find the man who can free my brother."

They stood there in the flickering candlelight, eyeing one another like a couple of dogs ready for a fight. Finally Lucy whinnied, and they broke eye contact. Rett scooped up Elizabeth's bag and started throwing her belongings into it. He just wadded her dress up—didn't even bother to fold it—and crammed it in.

"What are you doing?"

"I found a shelter. Of course, if you'd rather stay in the woods alone…"

"I might just do that. I'm an experienced camper. I have a gun, as you learned when you ambushed me. I'll be fine." Wait. Where was her gun?

He held the candle up and examined the bullet-scarred tree trunk, then looked at her. "Look, Miss Covington. You nearly killed me, but you didn't. Next time you shoot someone and miss, it could very well be the last thing you do. Now come with me." He walked away, holding the candle and leaving her in the pitch-black.

"Wait!" she called, and Rett stopped. "I...I dropped my gun."

There went the muttering again, and this time she was glad she couldn't understand his words.

"You've no right to be upset," she justified. "It's your fault I dropped it." It sounded reasonable to her, anyway.

Rett used her candle to relight his own, then handed hers back to her. They searched the area in silence, except for a hoot owl taunting her from a branch above. She had to find that gun before Rett did. If he found it first, he might not give it back.

There! The metal glinted in Rett's candlelight, and she scooted to get it before he could. He just stood there, watching her with a look she couldn't quite identify. Something between disgust and pity. Well, she'd show him. She didn't need his pity.

He turned around, mounted his horse—Bear, he'd called him—took Sugar's reins and rode into the darkness as if he knew where he was going. She looked around, for what little good it did her with no light, then untied Lucy's harness and followed him into who knew where.

Of all the blasted, confounded, harebrained schemes. Who did she think she was? What in the world was she thinking, pointing that gun at him? If they hadn't been on the verge of facing Hardy and his gang, he would have taken it from her. As it was, he wasn't sure he'd be able to protect her and capture Hardy both. She needed some form of defense. He just hoped she didn't use it on him.

And Herrington! Surely he knew she'd followed Rett. Or maybe not. Elizabeth Covington seemed the type to do exactly as she pleased when she set her mind to something. But that…that Cooper woman surely was behind this in some way. They were two of a kind, Elizabeth and Amelia Cooper. At least they hadn't both tagged along.

Why hadn't he made sure she was behind bars with her "brother" before he'd left Houston? Why hadn't he gone against Cody and Ray, followed through on his gut and put a stop to this whole thing before it started? But no. He wouldn't berate himself for her foolishness. The only thing he was guilty of was giving her credit for more common sense than she apparently possessed.

At the shelter—an old dugout someone had crafted long ago in the side of a hill—he tethered Bear and Sugar to a low branch and pushed aside the brush. He tossed his bag to one side, then lit another candle and placed it in a safe spot. Before long the area filled with a soft glow.

She stomped behind him, holding her own candle, looking around. Then she started moving stuff, straightening a branch, repositioning a half-rotted table, setting things up as only a woman would do. Fascinating. Why bother making things neat and pretty when they'd only sleep a few hours and leave first thing in the morning? But there she was, spreading out her bedroll until it was just so, using the candle and pulling stuff from her pack, then replacing it more neatly.

Ridiculous.

Rett looked out the entrance at her horse, bathed in moonlight. Nice. At least he could credit her with choosing a decent mount, though he had no way of knowing if she'd chosen the mare herself or if she'd been chosen for her.

He lay back, put his hands behind his head and watched the light flicker on the ceiling. *God, You said You'd give us wisdom. But how in the tarnation— Oh, sorry, God. Didn't mean to use that kind of language. But how in the world am I supposed to find Hardy and take care of Elizabeth at the same time?*

For a long time neither of them spoke. Finally he heard her settle into her bedroll, and he looked toward her. She was nearly ten feet from him, but he could see she lay on her side, her back to him. His heart quickened as he tried, unsuccessfully, not to study the soft curves of her silhouette. *Confound her.* Nothing but an unneeded, unwanted distraction.

After a time, he forced himself to roll onto his side, away from her. Good thing he'd packed plenty of coffee. He had a long night ahead of him, and now he didn't think he'd get a bit of sleep.

Elizabeth tossed and turned for hours before she finally slept. Oh, she wasn't nearly as frightened as she had been earlier. At least she had some shelter around her, crude as it was. Now she was just plain mad.

Deep down she knew she didn't have a right to be mad at Rett. After all, she was the one who'd nearly killed the poor guy. She knew her presence didn't make his job any easier. Nursing her fury, however, was better than the alternative. She was afraid if she didn't focus on her anger, her heart would center on all the things she found so alarmingly irresistible about the man. So she clung to her ire, as a matter of choice.

When she slept, her dreams were more disturbing than real life. She dreamed of Rett protecting her from some forest creature. Dreamed of him carrying her up the stairs at the hotel. Dreamed of him kissing her.

It was a most pleasant dream—that was the disturbing part. And when he shook her shoulders at dawn to awaken her, she stretched her arms catlike over her head and smiled at him. Smiled at him! Then she remembered everything and wiped that treasonous smile from her face and tried to wash the pleasant dream from her memory. What was wrong with her?

"Good morning," he said, and he didn't sound nearly as miffed as he had last night.

"Good morning," she replied, even as she realized she was in a most compromising position. She needed a privy. And there was no privy. She crawled from her bedroll, then stood and surveyed the little dugout. "I…uh…"

Rett grinned that annoying half-cocked grin of his as if he knew exactly what she needed but didn't want to make it easy for her. She searched for words, but her tongue seemed thick and unsure. Why did this man get under her skin so?

Finally, he took pity on her and pointed out the entry, toward a dense thicket of cedar. "I'll stay in here, and I'll even face the other way. Take your time. But be quick about it."

The nerve! But she wouldn't give him the satisfaction of knowing he'd embarrassed her. It would only encourage him. Instead, she simply nodded, spun around and pushed her way through the door and to the other side of the thicket until she was certain she had enough privacy.

She took a little more time than she needed, though, just to spite him.

Upon her return he nodded, tipped his hat and said, "Better get a move on. If the reports were right, Hardy's already quite a ways ahead of us."

Good thing she'd straightened her pack last night. In no time, she had her bedroll and carpetbag secured and climbed onto Lucy, only to find Rett watching her. Obviously, he hadn't expected her to be so efficient.

"I'm impressed. I wouldn't have taken you for the outdoors type."

"There's a lot about me that may surprise you, Ranger Smith."

There was little conversation for the next several hours. Rett was tired, and he was accustomed to such a life. He could only imagine how Elizabeth felt. Midday they rode into the town of Hemphill, Texas, and stopped at the sheriff's office. Maybe that man had heard something new about Hardy and his gang.

"Rumor has it they're hidin' near Alexandria," Sheriff Prewitt told him. "I'm waiting for backup, and I suggest you do the same. There's more than a half dozen of 'em."

Rett looked out the window to where Elizabeth stood, combing down Lucy, then Sugar. She even offered Bear a treat. If he could leave her here... "No time for that. I can't wait. You think you could hold that little lady in your jail till I get back?"

Prewitt scratched his head. "What's she done?"

"Nothing that I know of."

"So you want me to look after her so you can go get yourself shot? No, thanks."

"That's what I was afraid of. What's the quickest way to get there from here?"

"Head due east. You should be there by sundown. There's a little cabin southwest of town. My contact says they stayed there the last two nights. Hardy must be injured—he wouldn't stay put for any other reason. He knows we're on his tail."

Be there by sundown. What in the world would he do once he got there? He decided to try to talk some reason into Elizabeth. Little good it would do him, but he had to try.

"Much obliged." Rett tipped his hat to the sheriff and exited the small office. Elizabeth ignored him and continued coddling the horses. He almost envied the beasts. "If they stay put, we'll be on them by nightfall."

She didn't respond, at least not verbally. But her hand slowed where she brushed Lucy's coat, and she seemed to stop breathing for a moment.

"Look, Miss Covington. There's a nice little boardinghouse up the street. You could stay there, relax, maybe get some rest. Believe it or not, I'm actually pretty good at my job. Maybe this time tomorrow, we'll have the real Hardy in custody, and your brother can go free."

Now she looked at him, a vulnerability in her expression that broke his heart. "So you believe me?"

He thought his response through before he spoke. "I don't know. But I'm considering the possibility that you're right, and I've been wrong."

Her face hardened, the openness of a moment earlier vanished like a vapor.

"You're not getting rid of me that easily. I can come with you or I can follow you. Your choice."

Rett bit the inside of his cheek to keep from spilling the words he really wanted to say. Instead, he shook his head. "I wish I could help you understand the gravity of the situation."

"No one understands that better than I do, Ranger Smith. Evan is my only living relative. If I lose him, I'll be truly alone. Not to mention, this world will be robbed of one of the kindest, most decent men who's ever walked this earth. Evan is a rare, noble soul, and if he's hanged, it will be...it will be—" Her voice caught, and she turned away.

Rett reached a hand to stroke her back, to offer some form of comfort, but stopped just short of touching her. She wouldn't want comfort from the one responsible for her tears. Instead, he cleared his throat and said, "We'd best be going if we're going to make it before sundown."

Chapter 12

Well, at least she knew how to handle a horse, which was more than Rett had expected. She'd said she had training in equestrianism, but riding in some swanky ring with some fancy horse and wearing some elaborate getup was a far cry from what they were doing now. Still, she had certainly proved her mettle during the past few hours. They'd ridden hard and she'd kept up, without a single complaint.

Dark clouds dotted the horizon, and thunder grumbled in the distance. They needed to stop, but Rett didn't know how much good riding time they had left, so he pushed on. According to Prewitt, Hardy's suspected hideout wasn't far from here.

They pressed forward through the light drizzle that fell, even when it pelted harder and harder. But when lightning streaked the sky, Rett knew they should stop.

The last thing he needed was for one of the horses to spook. The problem was, where?

He trained his eye on the landscape, watching for any kind of beaten path. After a time and several close calls with lightning, he found one and followed it. As luck or Providence would have it, a dilapidated shack sat tucked away in the pines. Not much of a shelter, but at least it was a little better than the hovel they'd stayed in last night.

He rode Bear into the doorless lean-to and dismounted, then helped Elizabeth down from her horse.

Elizabeth's teeth chattered, and her lips looked blue. He tried to speak to her, but a rowdy clap of thunder sounded just outside the shack. Instead, he wrapped his blanket around her shoulders, grabbed his pack and motioned for her to follow him into the small cabin.

Once inside, he took a quick survey of the surroundings. A pile of ashes lay heaped in the fireplace, and a beat-up table and three stools took up space in the middle of the room. In one corner a straw mattress lay on the floor. Thick dust covered everything in sight; no one had been here in a while. To one side of the hearth sat a forgotten bottle of whiskey, cork in place.

Elizabeth saw it, too, a look of disgust on her pretty face. He thought about taking the bottle and draining it on the ground outside just so she'd know he wasn't a drinking man. But he thought better of it. After all, they were trespassing. Best leave things the way they found them.

"Have a seat," he yelled over the deafening rain.

She did, pulling his blanket closer around her shoulders. He had to hand it to her. Elizabeth was made of tougher stuff than he'd given her credit for.

Closer inspection of the room showed there was no firewood, and everything outside was soaked by now. They needed a fire—at least Elizabeth did. He could hear her teeth clack together, and her hair clung in sticky clumps to her face and neck.

As if reading his mind, she pointed to one of the rickety stools. "We could use that," she said, or at least, that was what he thought she said. It was difficult to hear over the howling wind and hammering rain.

Rett picked up the stool, turned it this way and that, then lifted it over his head and smashed it to the ground, shattering the wood into nice-size pieces of kindling. Paul Bunyan had nothing on him. As he bent over to pick up the pieces, he caught movement from his left, and he looked at Elizabeth. She covered her hand with her mouth and giggled like a schoolgirl. He wondered if she had any idea how attractive she was in that moment.

Elizabeth watched as Rett lifted the stool over his head like some kind of deranged caveman, then couldn't contain the squeak that escaped her as the stool crashed to the ground. For some reason, the whole thing struck her funny bone. Especially since there was an ax hanging right over the door.

He looked at her as if wondering what was so funny, and she pointed at the ax. When he caught sight of it, he shrugged and snorted, then kept gathering the pieces. She should probably help him, but right now her fingers were chilled to the bone and her whole body shivered, and she figured the best thing she could do was dry out a bit. Maybe she could make some dinner for them in return for his building the fire.

Rett said something, but she had a hard time hearing him over the earsplitting bellow from the heavens. The wind wailed, and she wondered if their little shelter might blow away. Rett pointed to the door, then held up his hand as if telling her to stay put. This was one time she didn't mind following orders.

He disappeared behind the door, and she pulled the blanket more snugly around her shoulders. A minute later, he reappeared with several more dry logs. Had they been in the lean-to? Must have been.

In no time, he motioned for her to move closer to the cozy fire as he rested against the wall on the other side of the hearth. There was no use trying to talk, at least until this storm let up. Instead, she rested her head against the dusty wall and soaked in the warmth of the flames. Before long her tired body gave in to weariness. She remembered wondering if that was her stomach or the thunder rumbling as her eyelids pulled down, heavier and heavier.

Rett watched Elizabeth's head tilt to the side, her eyes closed in deep sleep. Her mouth hung open slightly, and she looked like a child. A wave of something protective rose up in him, followed by another surge of frustration that she was even here.

But she *was* here, and like it or not, she was his responsibility. He'd taken an oath to serve and protect those who couldn't protect themselves, and she was one of those. Though she did seem to be full of surprises when it came to what she could and couldn't handle.

He watched her for a while until his stomach hollered at him. He had two cans of beans in his sack. He'd meant for that and the hardtack to last him three or four days. There were two more pieces of Sue's chicken, as well. He'd finished the cookies at breakfast, the rolls at lunch.

Her sack lay on its side next to her, and he wondered what provisions she'd brought. Should he investigate? No. Better leave her stuff well enough alone.

An iron skillet hung on a nail next to the hearth, and after a few swipes with the tail of his shirt, he opened one can of the beans and emptied them into the skillet, then set it on the ledge in the fireplace. At least they wouldn't have to eat cold beans. He lay the other food on the hearth so it could warm, as well.

Settling into a comfy spot against the wall, he watched Elizabeth sleep for a few more minutes. The whole scene was both relaxing and troubling, and before he knew it, he felt his own eyes sagging shut.

Next thing he knew, a searing pain shot through his hand and arm, and he awoke to find Elizabeth's boot pressed down on his fingers. "Ouch! My hand!"

"I'm sorry. Didn't mean to step on you. Did you place this skillet here? Whatever's in here is charred, but it tastes wonderful." She had some kind of brown fabric—perhaps the dress she'd worn earlier—wrapped around the skillet handle, which she held at arm's length.

The beans! The stench hit him for the first time, even as he sucked on his fingers to ease the pain from her boot heel. "Oh, yeah. I did put those there. I guess I fell asleep." He shook his fingers. "Sorry about that."

"Well, Ranger Smith. It looks like you need me for

something after all. Move out of the way, and let me fix us a real dinner. Or at least something better than burned beans."

"There's more food there. Help yourself." He gestured with his injured hand to the chicken.

He watched as she examined the contents of her carpetbag, went outside, then returned with a tin cup filled with fresh rainwater. She pulled out several small sacks of powder stuff. Was that flour? And something else. Before long, she was pounding out some type of doughy paste on the small table.

"Would you mind rinsing out the skillet?" she asked, and he sensed only the slightest bit of amusement in her tone. Her eyes, on the other hand, told him she knew that in this case she had the upper hand.

The skillet was now only slightly warm. As he opened the door, she called, "Where is the can from the beans?"

"The can?"

"Yes. The empty can. They did come from a can, didn't they?"

Rett nodded, wondering what in the world she wanted with an old empty can. He'd placed it in his pack to dispose of later. "In there." He pointed before heading onto the porch to rinse out the skillet in the still-pouring rain. At least the storm had slowed some.

When he reentered, she was using the can as a biscuit cutter. *Well, I'll be... Not bad for a city girl.* "Where did you learn to cook? I figured you probably had people to do that for you."

"As I said, Ranger Smith, there's a lot about me that might surprise you. My father wasn't a wealthy man when he was young, and he insisted that Evan and I learn real-life skills. Evan had to chop wood. I had to cook and do laundry." She lifted the circles of dough from the table and placed them in the skillet. "Oh, not all the time. If I were you, I'd reserve judgment on my cooking skills until you've tasted it. But Papa saw to it that our cook taught me the basics. Though I'm afraid Solomon thought I was more of a bother than anything else during those cooking lessons."

"Solomon?"

"The cook."

"The cook. I suppose you had a maid, a butler and a nanny, as well." The words were out before he could stop himself.

"As a matter of fact, we did. Wonderful people, all of them. Papa was grateful to be in a position to offer employment to such worthy individuals."

Rett had to admit, he'd never considered the idea that the wealthy actually provided income for people. He'd always thought of servants as frivolous.

Maybe it was the soft rhythm of rain on the roof or the flickering flames from the fireplace, but something about the setting called for quiet conversation. Despite his instincts screaming at him to keep things at a professional level, he pulled up a stool and watched as she worked the dough. "Tell me about your childhood."

Maybe it was the nap. Maybe it was the relief of the cool chill in the heated Texas summer or the steady rhythm as she mixed the dough, gently pressed it out, cut circles and filled the pan. Maybe it was the serenity of the scene, soothing her emotions from the jolts and jitters of the past few days. Whatever the reason,

Elizabeth found herself relaxing, much against her will. The last thing she wanted to do was let down her guard with this man. But that was exactly what she did.

"What would you like to know?"

"What would you like to tell me?" he asked, and his voice was husky and graveled.

"Not much to tell. I was loved. I was happy."

"I've not heard you mention your mother."

Knead. Press. Cut. She was almost out of dough, but they'd have enough biscuits for a couple of days. Who knew when they'd have a place to cook again? Elizabeth sighed. "I never knew her. She died when I was an infant. They say I look like her."

"She must have been quite a looker."

Elizabeth felt warmth in her cheeks and cast a quick glance at him before continuing her task. Was he red? Was he embarrassed he'd said that?

Surely not. Did Rangers get embarrassed?

"I'm tall like my father's side of the family. When I was thirteen, I tried on some of her dresses, and they barely reached my ankles." One by one, she placed the doughy circles in the skillet and moved them around so they'd fit. She'd have to make two pans.

"And your father? How long ago did he pass?"

Tears threatened, but she pushed them back. "Six months ago."

Rett didn't respond for a long moment. Finally, he said, "I'm sorry."

Elizabeth forced the lump in her throat back down to her stomach, forced her mind to happier thoughts. "Evan says Papa spoiled me. But I think he was the best father ever. I...I'm still finding my way without him. I'm not sure how to exist in a world without Papa. Everything just seems off balance."

Rett shifted on his stool and let out a weighty breath. "I know exactly what you mean. I had a twin sister. We used to play at the pond from morning to night. We'd hide and practice our birdcalls, then see if we could track the other down by listening. She was good, too. I often couldn't tell the difference between her and the real birds. Her favorite was the whip-poor-will." He leaned back, as if lost in time, and whistled the low *whip-poor-will, whip-poor-will* call. Elizabeth sat respectfully and didn't make a sound, for fear she'd startle him out of some cherished memory.

A moment passed, and he shook his head, as if he was pulling himself back to the present. "There was a long rope tied to a willow tree, and we'd swing from it and land in the middle of the pond. We'd have contests to see who could make the biggest splash. I was bigger, so I always won."

Elizabeth sat on her own stool and wondered where he was going with this story.

"When we were twelve, we changed the contest. We'd swing back and forth, see who could stay on the rope the longest before jumping in. She was at eight counts, and the rope was slowing. So she hung on with her hands and swung her legs out to give it more force. But she slipped and went flying just as the rope reached the other side. She hit her head on a rock…"

Rett seemed lost in his thoughts, almost as if he'd forgotten she was there. After a while he looked at her, the painful memory flickering his green eyes with dark brown.

"I'm so sorry."

"It was a long time ago. But I know what you meant by the world seeming off balance. That's how I felt for a long time after Laney was gone."

Silent understanding passed between them, and Rett watched her turn to check the biscuits. "Do you have other siblings?" she asked.

"Lisa and Eldon. Both younger." Rett leaned his elbows on the table.

"Laney and Lisa. Everett and Eldon. Nice names."

"Actually, the girls' names are Elaine and Elise. How did you know my name is Ev—?" He stopped himself. Blast that Sheriff Goodman.

"Don't you like your name? Because I think it's a perfectly lovely name. As a matter of fact, I think I'll use it from now on. Ranger Everett."

He could hear the teasing in her voice. It was good to see her like this. She'd been through a lot. "You can call me whatever you like, as long as you don't get yourself shot or killed."

"I don't plan to."

As quick as that, the tension returned, as if they'd both just remembered the reason for this trip. The rain had stopped. They didn't have much daylight left, and it didn't need to be wasted. "How long till those biscuits are done?"

"They're ready." She offered him one, hot from the skillet.

Not bad. Not quite to Sue's level of expertise, but then, she didn't have Sue's experience. "Delicious."

"Thank you." She took one herself, and he reminded her of the warm chicken. She spread the cloth on the table between them, set the skillet beside it, then surprised him. "Would it be all right if we prayed?"

Did she want him to pray out loud? At home they'd always prayed before meals, but he hadn't continued the habit. He wasn't sure why. Well, now was as good a time as any to resume the practice. He bowed his head, cleared his throat and said, "Dear Father. Thank You for this shelter and this meal. Keep us safe, and allow justice to prevail. Amen."

"Amen," she echoed, and they ate quickly and silently. Soon enough she gathered the leftover biscuits and a few other things, as if she knew without him telling her. It was time to go.

He stood, rubbed his belly. "Thank you for a delicious meal, Miss Covington."

"Thank you for sharing your chicken." There was an awkward silence, and he wondered if her thoughts mirrored his own prayers as they prepared to head into who knew what.

God, please don't let this be our last supper.

Chapter 13

Rett slowed his horse and waved her back. They'd traveled in silence for the hour since they'd left the cabin. His decision to leave Sugar there left her with mixed emotions, yet she knew they didn't need to keep up with an extra horse. They'd get her on their way back. She'd come in handy when they transported Hardy to Houston.

At least, that was the way she hoped it would all play out.

She pulled Lucy's reins and patted the horse's neck to soothe her. So far she'd been a good horse. "Don't fail me now, girl," she whispered.

In the distance, through a thick copse of pine, a campfire glowed ever so slightly. Hushed voices—men's voices—floated through the wood, but she couldn't make out the words.

Rett drew Bear to a halt, then climbed down. "Stay

here," he whispered. "Watch the horses. I can't risk taking them closer—if they make a sound, we'll be discovered. I'm going closer…see what I can learn. I'll be back."

For the first time since she'd met him, she decided to obey orders. This was their chance to capture Hardy and set Evan free. She didn't want to mess things up. Her breath caught, and her heart used the inside of her chest as a punching bag as she watched him steal away, watched him disappear into the dusk.

Could they hear her pulse as loudly as she could? Surely it was a distraction as it thrummed in her ears and echoed into the musky green timberland. She strained to hear, strained to make out their crude-sounding conversation, strained to catch a glimpse of Rett in the twilight. Bear whickered after his master, and Elizabeth dug into her pocket, pulled out two sugar cubes and offered one to each horse. Perhaps that would keep them quiet for a while.

Two eternities had passed when she heard a twig crack. She stiffened but didn't move. At long last Rett stepped around a tree and into view, his finger over his lips in an effort to keep her quiet. Well, he didn't have to worry. She wasn't saying a word. For the first time in her life, her ability to speak was paralyzed.

He crept as close to Lucy as he could and motioned for her to lean toward him. When her face was level with his, he whispered oh-so-quietly, "It's him. It has to be. You won't believe how much he looks like your brother."

She wanted to shout a hallelujah or sing in celebration or jump from her horse and dance a jig. They'd found him! Evan would be free!

But not yet. Though her spirit soared, she somehow kept her composure intact and nodded. *What now?* she mouthed silently.

"We wait for some of them to fall asleep. We'll never take them now. Our only chance is to catch them by surprise."

"How many are there?"

"Hardy and four more, that I could see. A couple of them are half-drunk and half-asleep, so they shouldn't be a problem."

That was a matter of opinion.

"You have your gun?"

She nodded.

"It's loaded?"

"It is now." She slipped the ammunition into its place. "I wish it took more than one bullet at a time. I'm not very fast at reloading."

Rett gave her a steely look. "Don't miss, then."

God help her.

"We'll tether the horses and I'll sneak around to the other side of their lair. It's an old tent. Makes the place we stayed earlier look like a palace. You stay here. No matter what happens, I want you to stay hidden. You have your gun. Only shoot if they capture me and come after you. Then, like I said, don't miss."

"Aye, aye, Cap'n." Exhilaration pulsed through her veins as she realized this was better than arguing in court any day. She might be the wrong gender for practicing law, but the covert capture of common criminals apparently wasn't chauvinistic. She felt wild and free, like when she and Evan played cowboys and Indians in the backyard. Only this wasn't a game. And the man up ahead wasn't Evan.

But wait. Why did she have to stay behind? She had more at stake than Rett. She should go. She didn't have to get too close, but she wanted to be there when Hardy was captured, wanted to see what was going on. She waited for Rett to steal out of sight, then tethered Lucy and followed him.

Rett flattened his belly into the forest floor and wished for the thousandth time he had Cody or Ray with him instead of Calamity Jane. At least he could rely on Elizabeth's intelligence, if not on her sharpshooting skills. He hoped she'd lassoed some common sense in the past few days and wouldn't try anything stupid. *God, help us both.*

The outlaws sat around a campfire and passed around a whiskey flask. All but Hardy, that was. He didn't touch the flask, which was unfortunate. Rett would have preferred to have the criminal's senses compromised. One of the men, a short, squatty fellow, told an off-color joke, and Rett wondered if Elizabeth had heard it. Once again, he wished he could protect her. Not only her life but her ears, as well. But she'd put herself in this situation…sort of. He supposed he was somewhat responsible, as well.

Behind the group, a crude tent had been set up. Not big enough for all of them, certainly. Must be Hardy's— he was clearly the boss. Rett studied Hardy's profile. It was uncanny how much he looked like the man sitting in the Houston jail. All except for the eyes. While Evan's eyes—yes, he was convinced the man in Houston was Evan Covington—were gentle and meek, Hardy's eyes fit his name: hard. Cold. And his face, though the features were similar, was more weathered than Evan's. They could pass as brothers for sure.

One by one, the drunken desperados fell asleep... all except Hardy. He sat there staring into the flames as if daring them to flicker out of turn. Considering the other men were inebriated and would surely sleep hard, Rett figured now was his chance. He skillfully, silently lifted himself from his position and stole forward. Leaves under his feet crackled, and Hardy looked in his direction. Rett froze. Hardy didn't move and eventually shifted his gaze back to the flames.

Warily, he crept onward, advancing on the ruthless renegade until he had him in his sights. He would never shoot an unarmed man, though he was tempted. Best get as close as possible, then make his presence known with the click of his rifle. He was just lifting himself from the ground when he heard a scream. Elizabeth!

He scrunched back down behind the brush and watched as a lone bandit dragged Elizabeth into the firelight.

"Well, well! What do we have here?" Hardy asked, a cruel smile forming on his hollow face. How had that happened? This new fellow must have been standing watch somewhere outside the camp. *Why her, God? Why couldn't he have found me instead?*

"Stop! You're hurting me!" Elizabeth yelled.

Without thinking, Rett stood, aimed and pulled back the hammer.

Pain seared through Elizabeth's arm at the rough grip of the oaf who had her in his clutches. "Let me go, you big dolt!" With all her might, she lifted her knee and let her boot heel crash down on the man's toe. He just laughed. His boots were thicker than hers.

"Look here, Jimmy boy! We're gonna have us some fun tonight."

Elizabeth gasped as she looked into the face of a man who looked unbelievably like Evan. This face resembled how Evan might look if he were a few years older and...and mean.

"Let her loose, Charlie. That's no way to treat a lady." Hardy's tone belied his words. He was no gentleman. Charlie loosened his grip but didn't let go. She thought of the Deringer in her boot but couldn't figure out how to retrieve it.

If only she hadn't felt the need to shift positions. She'd been lying perfectly still, barely breathing, when she got an itch. She'd tried to ignore it, but any time she'd ever tried to disregard an itch, it had only gotten worse. Ever so carefully, she had reached her arm back to scratch the place between her shoulders. Then, as she returned to her original position, the leaves beneath her rustled, and there was Charlie, pulling her to her feet and shoving her forward into the light.

Some of the sleeping men stirred, and in a moment two more of them were awake, rubbing their eyes and ogling her as if she were an apparition.

Something inside her knew she was in danger of a fate worse than death. She clawed and kicked and screamed like a cat in a dogfight, but the harder she fought, the tighter Charlie held her. The harder she fought, the harder the other men laughed. All except Hardy and one other fellow, one of the gang who seemed to eye her with a mixture of pity and shame.

Some unspoken voice inside her said if any one of those men was likely to help at all, it would be him.

She forced herself to be still and focus on that man's eyes. No use. He locked eyes with her for an instant, then turned away as if to block her out.

Where is Rett? Please, God. Please get me out of here. I know You don't want me to die this way. And Evan! If I die tonight, so will Evan.

"What are you doing here?" Hardy asked, and she pulled her eyes back to him. His flinted eyes were stony and cold, and she felt the skin on the back of her neck prickle. She tried to speak, but no sound would come out. For the first time in her life, she knew what it was like to be wholly petrified.

"Speak!" the man yelled, and she knew she'd better give him an answer. And it couldn't be the real one. Or could it?

"I...I was looking for you."

Hardy's eyebrows lifted, and he looked bemused. "For me?"

"Aren't you James Weston Hardy?"

"Yes. I believe I am. What do you want?"

"They've mistaken my brother for you. The resemblance is...uncanny. He's about to be hanged. I need to prove you're the real Hardy in order to save my brother."

The man chuckled, then stopped, then reared his head back and laughed out loud. Soon all the men were laughing, though she didn't see anything funny in what she'd said.

"What a tragic story. Tell me, ma'am. How can I assist you? Would you like me to ride back to the jail with you and turn myself in?" More laughter. "Or perhaps we can all go. Yes, that's it! We'll plan a heist and break my long-lost twin brother out of jail. It will be in all the papers. I'll be famous!" Hardy seemed quite amused with himself, and Elizabeth wanted to kick him. She thought better of it.

"Unfortunately for you, my dear, I'm already famous."

"*Notorious* is a better word."

"In my dictionary the two are the same." He walked a slow circle around her, looking her up and down like a jackal eyeing a wounded antelope. "Frank!"

"Yes, sir?" The man from earlier, the one she'd suspected might feel a little compassion, stepped forward.

"Take our guest into the tent and see that she's comfortable."

"Yes, sir." The man took her by the arm, gently but firmly, and led her into a dark tent.

"Please, mister. Frank, is it? Please don't do this. I can tell you're not like the rest of them. I can see it in your eyes. If you let me go, I promise I'll see that you get a fair trial. I promise I'll do all I can to make sure you don't hang with the rest of them. Please."

Rett circled a wide, slow girth around the camp as he watched the scene play out before him. He remembered Evan's request to care for his sister, felt a wash of protection and indignation, and something like... something like love well up inside him, and he knew he must save her. This was no longer about being a Ranger. It was about being a man.

He couldn't shoot now. There were too many of them. Even if he took one down, the others would come after him and kill him, and then they'd kill her. But not until they'd done a lot worse to her. *Please, God.*

He watched the average-size man, probably the youngest of the group, lead Elizabeth into the tent, and he knew he must act. He'd heard Hardy's orders and felt pretty certain the young lackey wouldn't mess with her. Hardy would go first, and the others would get what was left over. The thought made his stomach churn.

It was now or never. At least if he shot, it would divert attention away from Elizabeth and give her a chance to escape. If only he could communicate with her somehow, give a sign he was near. Surely she knew he wouldn't leave her, but she must be terrified. If he could only think of a way to reassure her before he shot. Maybe that would give her courage to run and not look back.

An idea whispered into his mind, and he didn't even think. Just acted with a careful pucker of his lips. *"Whip-poor-will. Whip-poor-will."* The sound echoed through the forest, but the men ignored it. Once more. Twice more. Maybe she'd get the message. Maybe.

Then he sighted in on Hardy and pulled the trigger. Chaos ensued, and he lost sight of the tent. In moments two men were nearly on him. He ran, but their bullets were quicker than he was. Searing pain blazed through his back and shoulder, and he was down. He could feel his consciousness leaving him… He fought to stay awake but knew it was a losing battle. Voices, voices all around him, behind him, beside him, past him. Voices…

Elizabeth heard the sound of the whip-poor-will and knew it was Rett. It had to be. Why would a bird be calling at this time of night? Owls, yes. Crickets? Of course. But a whip-poor-will?

She knew Rett was on the move. Before she could analyze the signal too much, a shot rang out, and the men outside started hollering. More shots fired. Rett! She tried to run, but Frank held her tight.

"Please. Let me go."

"You go out there now, you're gonna get shot."

"If I stay, worse will happen. Tell me it won't."

Frank kept hold of her arm with one hand and lifted the tent flap with the other. The voices seemed farther away. Rett! Had they gone after him? Was he dead?

Frank dropped the flap again and ran his free hand through his hair, as if contemplating his next course of action.

Elizabeth knew she had to think fast. "Uh…Mr…Frank?"

"Yeah."

"Is there a…privy nearby?"

He looked at her as if she'd left half her senses back in the woodlands. "A privy?"

"Yes. I must attend to a personal matter."

Dawning stretched across his face. "There ain't no privy."

Her face fell in practiced disappointment. She'd used it on Evan and Papa plenty of times, but they were used to her. With them it only worked if they wanted it to. But Frank was a new audience. She put on her saddest, most hurt face and prayed he'd be affected.

He lifted the tent flap again. "If you want, you can go behind that thicket. But I'll be right here, so don't try any funny business. If you get caught, it ain't gonna be pretty."

She smiled her prettiest smile. "Thank you, Frank." Then as an afterthought, she said, "You're not like them, you know. You could get away from here, start a new life for yourself."

He shook his head. "It's too late for me."

"It's never too late." Without another word, she lifted the flap, looked around and sneaked into the woods. She'd just stepped into the thicket, behind some trees, when the voices became stronger.

"Who's out there?"

"Some feller with a gun. He's dead now."

Dead? *Oh, God, no. Please, don't let it be so.*

"Where's his gun?" Hardy asked.

"Well…see, boss…we couldn't actually find him. We saw him shot, saw him fall. But when we went to look for him, it was too dark. We'll find him in the morning."

"We'll be gone in the morning. Somebody's sure to come looking for that fellow, and the girl, too. Frank! Where's the girl?"

"She…she went to the privy."

"The privy? You let her go? You simpleton!"

He let out a string of words that under normal circumstances would have made Elizabeth flush. But right now all she could think about was Rett. He couldn't be dead! *Oh, dear God. Please let him be alive.*

There was a lull, a murmur, and she strained to hear what was being said. After a minute or two, she made out three clear words. "Find the girl!"

Why had she stayed to listen? But she couldn't leave Rett. What if he wasn't dead? What if he was? She still wouldn't leave him. How an instant in time could contain so many thoughts, she didn't know. But in that instant, she cried out to the Almighty for wisdom and guidance as she never had before. *God, help me. Show me what to do. What do I do, God?*

As she prayed, she silently, stealthily crept through the woods, farther away from the camp. Her sense of direction wasn't great, and she took care to notice little landmarks to help her return, help her find Rett. Something pressed against her leg, as if heaven was sending a reminder. The gun.

Without a sound, she pulled the tiny Deringer from her boot. Good thing she'd loaded it earlier. Another bullet lay wedged against her ankle. The rest were in her bag.

Men's voices got closer. She pressed her back against one of the tall pines and prayed. Why was the moon so bright tonight? Surely they'd find her. As if in answer to her thoughts, a cloud moved over the moon, and for a time she was in complete darkness. Couldn't even see the glint of her handgun, which she held ready to shoot.

Breathe in…breathe out…slowly…no sound… She felt certain they could hear her, even as she prayed they wouldn't.

"Over here!" She recognized the man named Charlie, the one who'd found her first. "I think I heard something!"

What happened next was a matter of pure instinct, and perhaps pure Providence. She pointed her gun toward the voice, cocked the hammer and shot. Next she heard a loud thud and a groan, right in front of her! Something fell at her feet, and for a moment the clouds parted, and in the moonlight she recognized Charlie's blue plaid work shirt. Blood oozed from his back. His face was turned to the side, motionless. Had she killed him?

She covered her mouth to keep from screaming, even as her gut threatened to claw its way up her throat. Silently, only by the grace of God, she stepped over the man and picked her way through the forest. She couldn't run—not in these thick woods with no light. But at least she could move away from that awful scene.

After tripping and falling the third time, she decided it was a better choice to hide, remain quiet until morning. Perhaps she could move a few steps at a time when the moon moved into sight, but in this pitch-black there was no use trying.

After what seemed like hours but might have been only minutes, she heard the clopping of horse's hooves, and the angry voices receded farther and farther into the distance. She knew they'd left without her. *Thank you, God.*

Now to survive until daybreak. She felt totally helpless, totally alone. Hardy was gone. Rett was wounded or dead. And Evan would probably hang. Feeling in the dark, she found a rough pine and pressed her back to it, then slid to the ground. And she wept as if her soul had been torn in two.

Rett moaned. *Croaked* was a better word. His face was pressed against something prickly, and his head spun even though his eyes were closed. Where was he?

He tried to push himself up, but pain clawed through his shoulder and up his neck at the movement. And his arm. He couldn't feel his right arm.

Memories of the night before flashed through the

fog in his mind, and the dawning of realization was more painful than his shoulder. *Elizabeth!*

He opened his eyes, and the sunlight filtering through the trees told him he'd been out a long time. Too long. Still, if it was the last thing he did, even if he failed, he would try to find her. Try to save her. *Oh, God. Am I too late? Please don't let me be too late.*

Using both legs and his left arm, he pushed and heaved and struggled his way to a sitting position. Something foreign was wedged inside him; he could feel it every time he moved. He dragged himself to the nearest tree trunk, then leaned back and surveyed his surroundings. It looked different in the daylight. If only he could focus. If only... He leaned his head back against the tree just before everything went black again.

Chapter 14

Somehow she made it through the long, hollow night. There were no more tears; in their place was a vacant cavern where her emotions used to live.

Still, there was this need to keep going that superseded her emptiness. She must get back to civilization. She must find her way back to...the horses! That was where she'd go. But could she find her way? Would they even be there, or had those men stolen them? She thought of Sugar, but Sugar was one, maybe two hours from here.

Well, she'd never get anywhere sitting against a tree trunk. With effort, she pushed herself from the ground and tried to ignore the deluge of thoughts that swirled in her brain. She couldn't think about Rett lying dead. Couldn't picture Evan hanging from those awful gallows. The horses. She had to get to the horses. Which way?

Think, Elizabeth. Think. They'd left the horses tied in a small clearing. After that they hadn't gone very far. They had to be close. Did she dare call for them? What if those men heard her? What if…? She thought of Charlie. Was he really dead? What if he wasn't, and he heard her?

No. She wouldn't risk it. Not yet. She'd just have to do her best to figure out where in the world she was.

Sunlight filtered through the wispy pines and made patterns on the forest floor. Pine needles lay carelessly on the ground, dotted by pinecones of all sizes. She picked one up, studied its intricate pattern, then dropped it again. *Focus, Elizabeth.*

Looking up at the sky, she tried to place the sun. The forest was so thick she couldn't get a clear view. The shadows… Wasn't that what Papa had taught her? If you couldn't find the sun, look at which way the shadows fell. The way she faced, the shadows fell toward her. Her own shadow fell behind her. That meant the sun was somewhere in front of her. It was morning, and the sun rose in the…east. And they were headed east yesterday. So in order to retrace their path, she needed to turn around and go west…she thought. *Is that right, God? Help me. I'm not sure.*

In an effort to do something, anything, even though she wasn't sure it was the right thing, Elizabeth did an about-face and began a slow, careful trek through the piney woods. Every so often she stopped, reevaluated her position, tried to recall something from the night before that would help her and moved ahead again. She wasn't sure how long she journeyed that way, but of one thing she was certain: she didn't make the voyage alone. In and out of the towering trees, she felt an invisible hand guiding her, as if pulling her through a fog.

Finally, she heard something and nearly jumped out of her boots. There it was again…a whinny! Could it be? A few more steps, and a clearing opened up before her. Sure enough, there was Bear, looking at her as if to ask, *What took you so long?*

No sign of Lucy, though, other than a broken branch where she'd been tethered. The gunshots. Hadn't the liveryman said she spooked easily?

Slowly, softly, she sighed sweet nothings to the horse, now her only companion in the world. "It's you and me, Bear. I know I'm not your master, but will you help me find him?"

The horse nodded as if he understood, and somehow she believed he did. She looked around for any loose provisions and thought of her carpetbag. Had it been strapped to Lucy's saddle? No, there it was, at the base of a tree. She'd neglected to retie it before they'd left last night. Thank the Lord for small blessings. Rett's pack seemed securely in place, and she looped her own with his. Surely with both bags, there was enough there to tide her over until she could reach help.

After a moment more of brushing and soothing the mammoth paint horse, she hoisted herself into the saddle. Even as she spoke the command, she feared what she'd find if the horse obeyed. "C'mon, Bear. Let's go find Rett."

Rett drifted in and out of cognizance—he had no idea how long he'd been there. Each time he opened his eyes, he noted the placement of the sun, but next time he opened his eyes, he couldn't remember what he'd observed before. It was as if a mist invaded his mind, smothering his senses with a noxious fume.

Then he felt that cool hand on his cheek, heard that lovely, low voice saying his name, and he opened his eyes. For a moment he was caught up in the vision of her molasses curls bathed in sunlight, and he thought he was in some divine place. If this was his eternal home, it wasn't bad. Except for the pain… It was the pain that brought him back to reality, that reminded him he was indeed very much alive.

"Rett! Thank goodness you're still breathing. I was so afraid."

"You were afraid?" he rasped. "I thought you were dead. How did you escape?" The effort of conversation caused the throbbing to surge, and he caught his breath. But the sudden intake of air made it even worse, and he moaned.

"Don't talk," she whispered. "Bear and I will take care of you."

Bear? Good ole Bear. Somewhere in the distance he heard his trusty friend whinny before he collapsed into unconsciousness again.

Bear had taken her straight to Rett. He wasn't far away from where they'd left the horses, but with the thick pines, she didn't know if she could have found him on her own. He lay in a pool of blood, but thankfully, he was still breathing.

Next to him on the ground was his gun. *He's sure to want that.* Cautiously, she picked up the Colt revolver, removed the remaining five bullets, then thought better of it. She replaced three bullets but set the barrel at an empty slot just to be safe. Then she placed it in

Rett's holster. After last night, she didn't want either of them to be without defense in this wild country.

Elizabeth's nursing skills were limited, at best. But she knew she needed to find the source of blood flow and stop it, or he'd bleed to death. From the amount of blood on Rett's shirt and the ground around them, she was surprised he wasn't already dead.

At least he was unconscious. Maybe that would spare him the pain of her moving him around, jostling him this way and that, trying to find the bullet hole. Tenderly, she held him in place as she pulled one shoulder forward. There it was.

She lay him back as gingerly as possible and opened her bag. Finally, a worthy use for that blasted petticoat. She pulled it out and used a sharp stick to start a rip in the fabric. Strip by strip, she tore the despised garment into bandages, careful to keep them draped in her bag. The last thing he needed was to get an infection from dirty bandages.

She wished she had some of that carbolic acid the doctor had used on her, but at least she had water from the canteen. It was nearly full; they'd refilled in Hemphill. But she still needed to be careful.

She poured a bit of it onto one of the rags and, as gently as possible, cleaned up the wound. Rett moaned, and Bear whinnied. Cupping one hand, she poured some water into it and fed it to the horse. Then she sparingly washed her hands and began wrapping the bandages around Rett's arm and shoulder. For the first several layers, blood seeped through. But after the twelfth layer or so, the bleeding ceased, until the bandages on top remained dry. Now to get him to shelter. Could she find her way back to the cabin?

Probably not. But hopefully, Bear could. "Good boy," she whispered and stroked the horse's forehead. "You'll get us to safety, won't you?"

How would she ever transport this bear of a man? She was strong, yes...but not that strong. If she could somehow get him on his horse, she could walk alongside. It was clear he'd be no help; he was too far gone. She'd have to drag him to safety.

That was it! She'd drag him. What was it the Indians used? She closed her eyes and pictured the Wild West book Evan used to read to her. They carried things by placing them on some kind of stretcher, which they dragged behind the horse. A travois! That was what it was called.

Could she make one?

Of course she could. She didn't have a choice. A quick search of the area turned up some long branches, and she chose the three strongest. She'd form a triangle. Using some leftover bandage strips, she tied them together, wrapping the fabric around and around, winding it this way and that until the frame was secure. Now for some kind of support. She could use more branches, but she'd need a lot of them. Did she have enough bandages to tie them?

No. It wouldn't be enough. She needed something big that she could stretch across. Rett's pack had a blanket... She'd use that if she had to. But she'd need something to cover him with.

What else was there? Matches. Rope. Day-old biscuits. The sight of those reminded her how hungry she was, and she stuffed a large bite into her mouth as she kept searching. She moved from his pack to her own bag, though she didn't think there was anything there… Her dress! Yes, that would work. If she tied her dress to the frame, it could work as a lower support. She could save the blanket to provide warmth.

His pale face scared her… He'd lost too much blood. *Please, God. I know you are helping me. Please let him live. And please let the authorities believe me this time when I tell them Evan is my brother. I've seen Hardy with my own eyes. Please let them believe me.*

After careful placement of her dress, reinforced with the last strips of petticoat, she decided to wake Rett. Any help he could give her would be welcome. She laid the travois to his left in hopes he could maneuver himself onto it. Then she'd figure out how to use the rope to tie it to Bear.

"Hey, Ranger. Time to wake up." She whispered the words and lightly nudged him. Once again he moaned, and she held the canteen to his lips. "Drink," she said.

Cradling the back of his head with her other hand, she guided him to tilt his neck back and let the cool refreshment drizzle down his throat. Some of it spilled down his cheek, but that was okay. He swallowed, and she exhaled in relief.

"Rett, Bear and I are going to pull you to safety. I've made you a stretcher, but I need your help. It's right beside you. Can you move your body to the left?"

She'd built a travois? Incredible. Elizabeth Covington certainly wasn't like any other woman he'd met. It took all his strength to push himself onto his left arm and use his legs to scoot his body onto the crudely framed pallet. She hovered and helped the best she could. Once he was situated, she used rope to strap him in place.

As he lay there, Bear clopped near and nuzzled his face. "Hey, boy. Good boy." Rett could feel his awareness fading again, but he fought it. As long as he was awake, he could at least offer some assistance.

Soon she led Bear into position, and Rett could hear her working to secure the travois. Occasionally she jostled him, and each time it was followed by a profuse apology. "I'm so sorry! Did I hurt you? Please forgive me."

Truth was, he didn't think anything she did could possibly make the pain any worse. Then again, who was he kidding? He was about to be dragged and bumped for who knew how long. Maybe it would be better to pass out again.

At long last she knelt before him. "Rett, I'm going to try to get us to that cabin we stayed at during the storm. Can you tell me if we're pointed in the right direction?"

With effort, he opened his eyes, studied the sun, then pointed up over his head and a little to the left. She seemed to understand and mumbled a low "Thank you." The last thing he knew was an angry stab of pain screaming at his shoulder as they lurched forward, and then everything went black again.

Every shadow, every sound caused Elizabeth to tense. She knew the other men had ridden off, but Charlie? She'd shot him. Of that she was certain. But she didn't know if she'd killed him. What would she do if he came after her?

She'd shoot again if she had to. She fingered the Deringer, now in the front pocket of her denims, and prayed again she wouldn't have to use it. She didn't know what was worse: the thought that Charlie might still be alive or that he might be dead on her account.

And Rett. Thank the Lord Almighty he was still breathing, but for how long? Could she save him? Of that she wasn't sure. Maybe if she got him settled in the cabin, she could ride for help. But first things first…to find the cabin.

Somehow Bear seemed to know exactly where he was supposed to go. After a time, they came upon another clearing, and there it was. As beautiful a site as any she'd seen, despite its crude structure and dilapidated state. And there, waiting right where they'd left her, tied to a long lead rope and chewing on a juicy clump of grass, was Sugar. The mare whickered a welcome and continued chomping her morsels.

Bear walked right up to the door, as if he knew to get his master as close as possible. Elizabeth climbed down and checked on her patient. Not good. Blood now seeped through the layers of bandages. How would she get him inside?

If Bear could have fit inside the doorway, she'd have let the horse pull Rett all the way into the house. But that would never work. She'd have to drag him in herself. She could do it. For once she was truly grateful for her size. She might not be dainty, but dainty wouldn't get her very far in this situation.

After propping the door open, she loosened the ropes from the saddle and draped them across her chest. With a great heave she pulled, inch by inch, until Rett was all the way inside the cabin. He groaned, but she ignored it for now. She had to clean that wound again. There was nothing left to use for bandages. She'd have to wash these and reuse them.

Near the lean-to, she found an old deep pot. It had collected rain from last night's storm. Perfect. It was heavy, but somehow she managed to transport it into the cabin without sloshing too much of the contents on the ground. Now for a fire. Hadn't she seen matches somewhere?

Rett's pack.

She gathered some stray pieces of kindling left over from yesterday's fire. Before long she had a blazing flame. Lifting his arm, she tenderly unwound the bloody bandages, dropping each one in the pot as she went. The moaning continued until finally, Rett opened his eyes.

"Where are we?"

"Back at the cabin."

"Hardy?"

"He got away."

She diligently kept at her task, despite the fact that blood had always made her queasy. But she had to be courageous. Papa once said courage wasn't the absence of fear; it was the decision to act in spite of that fear. Well, if that was the standard, she could certainly claim courage during the past twenty-four hours. The past week, really.

"Elizabeth." Rett pulled her mind from Papa's words. "You're going to have to cut the bullet out."

What? No. It was one thing to wrap a wound. But to take a knife and cut a man open? No. She'd ride for a doctor.

"Did you hear me?" Rett rasped.

"Yes, I heard you. But I'm about to leave. I'm sure Bear can lead me to Hemphill. I'll bring a doctor back with me, or at least someone who knows what they're doing. You don't want me cutting on you."

"You have to. It's been in there too long as it is. You can do it. I'll guide you through."

"How are you going to do that if you're passed out from the pain?"

"I won't pass out. Please. You have to, or I'll die."

The wind chose that moment to howl a warning, though whether it warned her not to play doctor or warned her to do as Rett said, she didn't know. But one way or another, he was a dying man. If he wanted her to... Goodness. Could she do it?

She'd have to. Courage.

"All right. Tell me what to do."

Rett turned his head toward the flames. "I see you started a fire. Nice job." His voice was weak—weaker than it was before.

"Get my knife. It's in my boot."

She did as instructed.

"Hold it over the flame to sterilize it."

Again, she followed orders.

"Now set it on the hearth, and help me out of my shirt."

Her face heated, but she ignored the feeling. Now was no time for propriety. As gently as possible, she helped him out of the bloody mess.

"I'm going to roll onto my stomach. You may need to help me," he rasped, and she felt bad he was doing all the talking. But she needed him to guide her through this.

"Now get that bottle of whiskey by the hearth."

"Whiskey?" She'd never touched alcohol before. Had no desire to now.

"It's not to drink. Pour it on my wound."

Of course. Alcohol. Perhaps there was a noble use

for the dreadful stuff after all. She pulled the cork, and the stench of it made her eyes water. Then she remembered Doc's pencil and set the bottle down. "I'll be right back."

He didn't respond, just lay there and waited. She exited the cabin, found a nice-size stick and returned. "Bite down on this."

He opened his mouth wide enough for her to insert the stick.

Then she took one of the hot, wet bandages and wrung it out to use as a rag. "You ready?"

The slightest nod told her to go ahead. He gasped when the antiseptic liquid touched the wound, but other than the tiniest flinch, he didn't move.

After a moment, his tense muscles relaxed just a bit. "Now reheat the knife. It needs to be hot." He spoke around the stick in his mouth, but she understood.

"But won't it—?"

He dropped the stick. "Yes. It's gonna burn. And it will smell awful. But the heat will help stop the blood flow and keep it from getting septic later."

Well, if he could handle the pain, surely she could handle the gruesome nature of the task.

"Locate the source of the blood flow. Use your fingers to press around—see if you can find the bullet. When you do, use the blade to dig it out."

She could feel the blood draining from her own face and wondered if she was paler than he was.

"Wait. Before you start…do you have a needle and thread with you?"

"Yes, in my bag."

"Good. When you've dug the bullet out, you'll need to sew me up."

Sew him up. More blood. *But that's okay, God. As long as You'll let this man live, I'll do whatever You ask of me.*

And then she proceeded to do something more wild and rugged, yet more tender and civilized, than she ever imagined. As she worked, she prayed. Each time she felt her valor waning, she drew strength from the source of courage.

Somewhere during that long, harrowing procedure, Rett lost consciousness. And somewhere along the way, as she cut and sewed and bathed and bandaged, Elizabeth gained the realization that she was deeply in love with this man.

Chapter 15

Rett awoke on his stomach. Would the pain ever go away? He tried to move, testing his shoulder. Gone was the intense foreign pressure just below his right shoulder blade. Elizabeth must have gotten the bullet out. Where was she?

"Hello?" he called, but silence was the only answer. His eyes closed again as he tried to recall a hushed conversation… Was that a dream? Had she said she was going for a doctor? Back to Hemphill?

Maybe it wasn't a dream. It seemed real but hazy. But if the words had really happened, had he imagined the tender kiss on his cheek? Or was that real, too?

No point trying to analyze it now. She was gone, and either she'd be back or she wouldn't. At least now, from what he could tell, he'd live.

Had she really done everything he'd asked of her? Poor thing. Imagine a city girl like that, accustomed to being coddled and cared for, having to do something so harsh. What a woman. He could spend the rest of his days with a woman like that. But of course, she'd never feel that way about him. How could she, after all that had happened?

God, I know I've not been in the habit of praying much, until lately. I'm not sure if I should talk to You about a woman, but I remember hearing we're supposed to talk to You about anything. Everything. I also remember that verse from childhood... How did it go? "Delight thyself also in the Lord; and He shall give thee the desires of thine heart," Psalm 37:4.

Lord, I'm not sure what it means to delight in You. But I sure promise to try. If it means obeying You and serving You and doing my best to please You, Lord, I give You my word. I'm Yours, no matter what the future holds. I know You've brought me through this alive.

But, Lord, if You're interested, I'd just like to say that my heart longs for Elizabeth. I'd really like it if she were mine. Any help You can give me there, I'd sure appreciate it.

He closed his eyes again, not sure if that prayer was appropriate but somehow knowing in his spirit that God heard, and He cared.

Elizabeth decided Bear could use a break. Besides, she missed Sugar. Lucy had been great before she escaped, but Elizabeth didn't feel the same oneness with Lucy as with Sugar. Now she felt as if she was home in the saddle. Sugar might as well have spoken English, the way she understood Elizabeth's commands. The mare had the sense of direction she lacked, and when

Elizabeth pointed her in the direction she thought might be Hemphill and said, "Take me to town," the horse whinnied and trotted forward.

Soon Elizabeth leaned forward, gave Sugar her head and prayed as she'd never prayed before. Somehow, with the wind whipping through her hair, she felt enveloped in God's love and care. During that trip from the cabin to town, Elizabeth laid down her worries, even as she realized that laying them down was not something she could do once, but rather, it was a daily moment-by-moment task. She decided that day that although she was afraid, she would trust in God's goodness.

Once on the main square, she didn't know whether to seek out the doctor or the sheriff first. A sign hung outside a tidy building: Richard Green, MD Physician and Magistrate. Well, since she was here, she might as well try the doctor first. She knocked, then pushed open the door without waiting for an answer. "Hello?" she called.

A matronly nurse peered at her over wire spectacles. "May I help you?"

"I'm looking for the doctor."

"You'll find him at the sheriff's office."

Well, that was convenient. Elizabeth thanked the woman and left Sugar tied to a post. The sheriff's office was just a few doors down.

Inside, a dignified gray-haired gentleman leaned back in a chair, feet propped on a desk. He wore no badge.

"Are you the sheriff?"

"No, but I'm filling in for him. James Weston Hardy has been spotted near here, and Sheriff Prewitt and a few others have gone looking for him. Is there anything I can do for you?"

Elizabeth spilled the story so fast she wasn't sure if the doctor could follow it. She sputtered and stammered, wrung her hands and twisted her braid. Not her best speech at all, but she'd never been in this kind of life-and-death situation before. Finally, she said, "The Ranger may die if he doesn't get proper medical care. Can you come?"

The man had already pushed back from the desk, grabbed his black doctor's case and gotten halfway to the door by the time she finished. "Take me to him."

Rett awoke before his eyes opened, to horse's hooves pounding outside the cabin. Men shouting. The cabin door banging open, then furniture moving. He dragged his eyelids until they released... There was a man hovering at the window. He looked to be wounded, but he aimed a Paterson revolver and shot, then ducked. Rett knew enough to keep quiet, for it seemed the man didn't know of Rett's presence. Best to keep his eyes shut and pretend to be asleep or dead.

More shouting outside. "Come on out! We've got the place surrounded."

"You ain't gonna take me alive!" the wounded man yelled and shot again. Rett recognized the voice as belonging to the man who'd dragged Elizabeth from the woods. Eyes still closed, Rett's mind scanned the possibilities. Wounded or not, he wasn't about to let this reprobate get away.

His gun... Was it still in his holster? He could feel the holster on his hip but didn't remember returning his gun to it. The knife... Elizabeth had used it to perform surgery. It was probably clear across the room. More shouting, and Rett took the opportunity to feel with his left arm… Yes. His gun was there. The noise stopped, and Rett froze.

For the next half hour, the shooting and shouting continued, with sporadic breaks in the chaos. Each time the noise escalated, Rett eased a little more of his gun out. Finally, he had the weapon out and ready. Now he just had to wait for the right opportunity.

The man had to be running out of bullets. He'd counted four shots, and he knew that model held only five bullets. So after the next shot was fired, Rett gritted his teeth, strained toward the man with his good arm, readied the barrel. The unmistakable click-click-click of a cocked Colt Single Action Army got the man's attention, and he swung his neck, clearly startled by Rett's presence.

"Drop your weapon," Rett called with as much force as he could muster. Instead, the man pointed the Paterson directly at him and pulled the trigger. Nothing.

A look of terror enveloped the man's face. He tossed the gun to the side and lunged for Rett, but his injury prevented him from hitting his mark. Rett shot, but the barrel was empty. What? There should be five more bullets!

The man moved closer, and Rett shot again. Another blank.

Once again, the lowlife heaved forward, and Rett shot once more. This time, the bullet hit its mark, and the man yelped in protest. That criminal wouldn't be using his shooting arm for a good long time.

The door banged open, and Sheriff Prewitt burst in,

followed by several other badge wearers, all pointing barrels at the man crying on the floor. Rett collapsed at his place and closed his eyes. More shouting. More horses. Was that Elizabeth's voice?

"Rett! What happened? I leave you alone for a couple of hours, and you have another gunfight? What am I going to do with you?" Something wet landed on his cheeks, and he opened his eyes to see the most beautiful face he'd ever seen.

Elizabeth. And she was crying.

Elizabeth couldn't cork the tears that flowed from somewhere deep inside. When she'd heard that final shot as she approached the cabin, she'd been so afraid...

Now relief deluged her. Relief that she hadn't killed Charlie. Relief that he was in custody, riding away with the sheriff, in handcuffs and draped over a horse. Relief the sheriff had told her he'd already wired Houston, informing the authorities that Hardy had been spotted in the area. He'd even shown her the return wire, stating that Evan Covington had been released from custody.

And finally, relief that Rett was still alive. She moved aside to let Dr. Green examine her patient.

With his good arm, Rett reached for her. "Elizabeth," he whispered, and in that one word were a thousand messages of gratitude. Of relief.

Of love.

"I...I don't know if this is the time or place," he strained to say.

"Shhh," she told him. "We'll have time to talk later."

"I don't want to wait. You...you saved my life."

"You would have done the same for me."

"I don't know how to thank you."

"You can get better."

He squeezed her hand, drew her closer to him. "Elizabeth."

"Yes?"

"I love you."

The tears she thought she'd managed to contain engulfed her again, and she fought to speak the next words so he could understand them. "I love you, too."

"Will you marry me?"

"Yes!"

Dr. Green cleared his throat, as if to remind them they weren't alone. Elizabeth felt heat crawl up her neck and ears, but she didn't care. Rett loved her. She loved him. And Evan was a free man.

"Miss Covington, I must say, you did a fine job caring for your patient." Dr. Green wiped down his tools and replaced them in his bag. "The wound looks like it will heal in time. Just keep it clean and dry. He'll be ready to travel in about a week."

A week. Well…she hadn't thought about staying past today. What would she…? How would he…?

"Might I make a suggestion?" the doctor asked.

"I'm not only the local physician. I'm also the magistrate. Since you two seem set on getting married, and since he's going to need a nurse…I could perform the ceremony right now."

Rett looked at her, hope in his eyes. "I'd be honored if you would. It would make me the happiest man in the world."

She wanted to hug him tightly, but she didn't want

to cause him more pain. Instead, she squeezed his hand and said, "I'm the one who's honored."

And there, in front of a low fire, in a crude cabin in the Piney Woods of East Texas, Elizabeth Covington became Mrs. Everett Smith.

Ten days later, Elizabeth and Rett rode into Houston on a stagecoach. In place of the scaffold there hung a banner that read Welcome, Mr. and Mrs. Smith. A large crowd gathered at the center of town, and a cheer exploded as the lovebirds stepped onto the platform.

Evan was the first to come forward, and he wrapped Elizabeth in a tight hug before shaking his new brother-in-law's hand. Amelia was right behind, and from the way those two made eyes at each other, Elizabeth wondered if more wedding bells would soon sound.

Mr. Herrington harrumphed from behind Evan. "Well done, Miss Covington. Well done. If you'd still like a job as my assistant, the position is yours."

"I believe she's already spoken for with a competing law agency," Evan interrupted, and Elizabeth smiled at one, then the other. It was one of the rare times she didn't know what to say.

Herrington clapped the younger man on the back in a good-natured ribbing. "Perhaps we should open Herrington and Covington, Attorneys at Law. Then we can both have her."

Evan laughed. "Make it Covington and Herrington, and I'll consider it."

Rett wrapped his good arm around her. "Sorry, gentlemen. She might be available to help you at some point in the future, but I'm afraid I'm going to need her nursing skills, to aid in my recovery for quite some time."

Elizabeth grinned, ignored the blush she knew blazed on her cheeks and turned to kiss the man she loved with all her heart.

* * * * *

REQUEST YOUR FREE BOOKS!

2 FREE INSPIRATIONAL NOVELS
PLUS 2
FREE
MYSTERY GIFTS

Love Inspired

YES! Please send me 2 FREE Love Inspired® novels and my 2 FREE mystery gifts (gifts are worth about $10). After receiving them, if I don't wish to receive any more books, I can return the shipping statement marked "cancel." If I don't cancel, I will receive 6 brand-new novels every month and be billed just $4.74 per book in the U.S. or $5.24 per book in Canada. That's a savings of at least 21% off the cover price. It's quite a bargain! Shipping and handling is just 50¢ per book in the U.S. and 75¢ per book in Canada.* I understand that accepting the 2 free books and gifts places me under no obligation to buy anything. I can always return a shipment and cancel at any time. Even if I never buy another book, the two free books and gifts are mine to keep forever.

105/305 IDN F49N

Name	(PLEASE PRINT)
Address	Apt. #
City	State/Prov.	Zip/Postal Code

Signature (if under 18, a parent or guardian must sign)

Mail to the **Harlequin®** Reader Service:
IN U.S.A.: P.O. Box 1867, Buffalo, NY 14240-1867
IN CANADA: P.O. Box 609, Fort Erie, Ontario L2A 5X3

Are you a subscriber to Love Inspired books
and want to receive the larger-print edition?
Call 1-800-873-8635 or visit www.ReaderService.com.

* Terms and prices subject to change without notice. Prices do not include applicable taxes. Sales tax applicable in N.Y. Canadian residents will be charged applicable taxes. Offer not valid in Quebec. This offer is limited to one order per household. Not valid for current subscribers to Love Inspired books. All orders subject to credit approval. Credit or debit balances in a customer's account(s) may be offset by any other outstanding balance owed by or to the customer. Please allow 4 to 6 weeks for delivery. Offer available while quantities last.

Your Privacy—The Harlequin® Reader Service is committed to protecting your privacy. Our Privacy Policy is available online at www.ReaderService.com or upon request from the Harlequin Reader Service.

We make a portion of our mailing list available to reputable third parties that offer products we believe may interest you. If you prefer that we not exchange your name with third parties, or if you wish to clarify or modify your communication preferences, please visit us at www.ReaderService.com/consumerchoice or write to us at Harlequin Reader Service Preference Service, P.O. Box 9062, Buffalo, NY 14269. Include your complete name and address.

LIDIR13R

REQUEST YOUR FREE BOOKS!

2 FREE INSPIRATIONAL NOVELS
PLUS 2
FREE
MYSTERY GIFTS

Love Inspired.
HISTORICAL
INSPIRATIONAL HISTORICAL ROMANCE

YES! Please send me 2 FREE Love Inspired® Historical novels and my 2 FREE mystery gifts (gifts are worth about $10). After receiving them, if I don't wish to receive any more books, I can return the shipping statement marked "cancel." If I don't cancel, I will receive 4 brand-new novels every month and be billed just $4.74 per book in the U.S. or $5.24 per book in Canada. That's a savings of at least 21% off the cover price. It's quite a bargain! Shipping and handling is just 50¢ per book in the U.S. and 75¢ per book in Canada.* I understand that accepting the 2 free books and gifts places me under no obligation to buy anything. I can always return a shipment and cancel at any time. Even if I never buy another book, the two free books and gifts are mine to keep forever.

102/302 IDN F5CY

Name	(PLEASE PRINT)	
Address		Apt. #
City	State/Prov.	Zip/Postal Code

Signature (if under 18, a parent or guardian must sign)

Mail to the Harlequin® Reader Service:
IN U.S.A.: P.O. Box 1867, Buffalo, NY 14240-1867
IN CANADA: P.O. Box 609, Fort Erie, Ontario L2A 5X3

Want to try two free books from another series?
Call 1-800-873-8635 or visit www.ReaderService.com.

* Terms and prices subject to change without notice. Prices do not include applicable taxes. Sales tax applicable in N.Y. Canadian residents will be charged applicable taxes. Offer not valid in Quebec. This offer is limited to one order per household. Not valid for current subscribers to Love Inspired Historical books. All orders subject to credit approval. Credit or debit balances in a customer's account(s) may be offset by any other outstanding balance owed by or to the customer. Please allow 4 to 6 weeks for delivery. Offer available while quantities last.

Your Privacy—The Harlequin® Reader Service is committed to protecting your privacy. Our Privacy Policy is available online at www.ReaderService.com or upon request from the Harlequin Reader Service.

We make a portion of our mailing list available to reputable third parties that offer products we believe may interest you. If you prefer that we not exchange your name with third parties, or if you wish to clarify or modify your communication preferences, please visit us at www.ReaderService.com/consumerschoice or write to us at Harlequin Reader Service Preference Service, P.O. Box 9062, Buffalo, NY 14269. Include your complete name and address.

LIHDIR13R

REQUEST YOUR FREE BOOKS!
2 FREE RIVETING INSPIRATIONAL NOVELS
PLUS 2 FREE MYSTERY GIFTS

Love Inspired®
SUSPENSE

YES! Please send me 2 FREE Love Inspired® Suspense novels and my 2 FREE mystery gifts (gifts are worth about $10). After receiving them, if I don't wish to receive any more books, I can return the shipping statement marked "cancel." If I don't cancel, I will receive 4 brand-new novels every month and be billed just $4.74 per book in the U.S. or $5.24 per book in Canada. That's a savings of at least 21% off the cover price. It's quite a bargain! Shipping and handling is just 50¢ per book in the U.S. and 75¢ per book in Canada.* I understand that accepting the 2 free books and gifts places me under no obligation to buy anything. I can always return a shipment and cancel at any time. Even if I never buy another book, the two free books and gifts are mine to keep forever.

123/323 IDN F5AN

Name _____ (PLEASE PRINT)

Address _____ Apt. #

City _____ State/Prov. _____ Zip/Postal Code

Signature (if under 18, a parent or guardian must sign) _____

Mail to the Harlequin® Reader Service:
IN U.S.A.: P.O. Box 1867, Buffalo, NY 14240-1867
IN CANADA: P.O. Box 609, Fort Erie, Ontario L2A 5X3

Are you a current subscriber to Love Inspired Suspense books and want to receive the larger-print edition?
Call 1-800-873-8635 or visit www.ReaderService.com.

* Terms and prices subject to change without notice. Prices do not include applicable taxes. Sales tax applicable in N.Y. Canadian residents will be charged applicable taxes. Offer not valid in Quebec. This offer is limited to one order per household. Not valid for current subscribers to Love Inspired Suspense books. All orders subject to credit approval. Credit or debit balances in a customer's account(s) may be offset by any other outstanding balance owed by or to the customer. Please allow 4 to 6 weeks for delivery. Offer available while quantities last.

Your Privacy—The Harlequin® Reader Service is committed to protecting your privacy. Our Privacy Policy is available online at www.ReaderService.com or upon request from the Harlequin Reader Service.

We make a portion of our mailing list available to reputable third parties that offer products we believe may interest you. If you prefer that we not exchange your name with third parties, or if you wish to clarify or modify your communication preferences, please visit us at www.ReaderService.com/consumerschoice or write to us at Harlequin Reader Service Preference Service, P.O. Box 9062, Buffalo, NY 14269. Include your complete name and address.

LISDIR13R